TOUGH

TOUCH

TOUGH

AMY HEAD

VICTORIA UNIVERSITY PRESS

TE WHARE WĀNANGA O TE ŪPOKO O TE IKA A MĀUI

VICTORIA UNIVERSITY PRESS
Victoria University of Wellington
PO Box 600 Wellington
vup.victoria.ac.nz

National Library of New Zealand Cataloguing-in-Publication Data

Head, Amy.
Tough / Amy Head.
ISBN 978-0-86473-893-6
I. Head, Amy. II. Title.
NZ823.3—dc 23

The following stories have been published previously:
'The Kitchen Pig Smokes the Mouseketeers' (*Sport* 39);
'Tough' (*JAAM* 30).

Printed by Printstop, Wellington

To Marleen and Mick

CONTENTS

CONTENTS

WEST COAST ROAD

Mr Edward Dobson, engineer, landed in Port Cooper in 1850 aboard the *Cressy*. He faced his first geographical obstacle in a range of hills that separated Banks Peninsula from the rest of Canterbury, the Port Hills. From the bridle path, the province descended into the Canterbury plains, supplied with plentiful water from alluvial aquifers: more than plentiful, excessive; they were swampy and flood prone. More and more settlers crossed the Port Hills to take up land and establish farms on the other side, and men like Dobson, men entrusted with the infrastructure of the province, went about building stopbanks and realigning the Waimakariri River to avoid inundation. A person who followed this river across the plains to its source would reach the Southern Alps, which sliced the island and the province into east and west. Dobson established himself an office in the amphitheatre of Lyttelton, a house within the four main avenues of Christchurch, and a sod cottage at Sumner, where a valley at the edge of the peninsula opened out to the sea.

In one of the first winters of the 1860s, Dobson invited Julius von Haast to the Sumner cottage. Provincial Engineer and Provincial Geologist, together they were planning a rail tunnel through the Port Hills. Dobson found a place for Haast's horse in their barn, out of the path of the strengthening southerly, and then led him in a brief but bitingly cold tour that took in the cows and chickens, the garden, and the recently added windows. The conditions were primitive beside London and Bonn, but what Dobson's household had to offer over and above all else, Dobson knew, was indoors, walking and talking. An evening with family would please Haast especially, who had been widowed in Germany and left a son behind.

How-do-you-dos and handshakes taken care of and glasses filled, Dobson offered Haast a comfortable seat and watched him take in the floor clock, the oriental rug where two of the children were cutting out shapes for a magic lantern show, and the upright, where his eldest daughter Mary was stationed. There was a rumpus underway upstairs, where Mrs Dobson was settling the youngest children. All in all it was a cosy domestic scene, but Dobson noticed Haast raise his fingertips to his temples, bowing his head to meet them. 'Mary, would you help with the babies?' he said. His daughter parted from her sheet music and crossed over to the door. Her frank, even face reminded Dobson of his mother. 'She's a good girl,' he told Haast, whose head swivelled to follow her progress until the door had closed behind her.

'My sons here would like to hear about your survey

in Nelson,' Dobson said. His eldest sons, straight-backed, were drinking their beers through shrubberies of beard. Haast obliged, describing how they had swagged food and equipment, horseless, through the virgin terrain, fighting Wild Irishmen, Lawyers, and Spaniards, so thick and entangling, the way he described them, that the party had to chop a path, foot by painstaking foot, as they went. With his fingernails so neatly trimmed, Haast didn't look to Dobson like the adventuring type.

'How did you manage your provisions?' Arthur asked. He was the eldest but for George. They were both surveying on the tunnel project.

'At the beginning I had everything: jams, tongue in tins, coffee. At the end? Oatmeal porridge, the same as everybody. Biscuits in soup.' Haast gulped the last of his glass. Dobson watched Arthur, who wasn't normally attentive to such details, pick up the bottle from the side table to refill it for him.

• • •

Tunnellers were still blasting through the extinct volcano between Christchurch and Lyttelton when, late in the summer of 1864, Dobson greeted Mary and Haast at the door. He did it partly out of affection, partly to arrange a tub of water for the horses, and partly to inspect the design of Haast's new coach. He kissed Mary, shook hands with Haast, and followed them inside.

Haast was narrating the nor'wester for Mary. 'First I rush off the Tasman Sea onto the West Coast. See how heavy I am with water.' He lifted his arms and let them sag, straining with the weight. 'Then, wait! I am obstructed by the Alps.' For the Alps he used the back of the settee. He dropped rain with his fingers. 'I fall on the rainforests and the ranges, fill the creeks and gullies, and now the ground is ready for all the unusual varieties of flora.' He lifted his arms, lighter now, higher, high enough to surmount the settee. 'Warm and dry, I sweep down onto the Canterbury Plains –' (the floral-patterned seat) '– and how do you say it? I rattle the people who live here. I make the horses thirsty.'

Through the window the spaniels overlapped on the lawn. While Dobson waited for Haast to finish, the youngest children, tottering by now, rounded the side of the cottage and the dogs rearranged themselves onto all fours, tails wagging. That morning, Dobson had heard their youngest, three years old, calling, 'Ring the bell for the children, dear!'

'Please sit down, everyone. Sit down,' Mrs Dobson was saying. Haast had finally brought his wind arms down to rest on Mary's shoulders. 'Give your jacket to Ettie, Julius, you must be overheating.' Julius was, quite visibly, and he did. He even unbuttoned his waistcoat.

Of course, the couple wanted to hear about Arthur's months surveying on the western coast – 'the wet coast' they often called it. While Arthur spoke, Dobson saw his son dressed only in flannels, clutching the rigging as roller after roller pushed his schooner sideways over the Grey River bar. At least five surveyors had drowned in the past year. But Dobson had high hopes for his second born, who seemed to create his own opportunities. He rubbed the lenses of his spectacles between his thumb and index finger with the handkerchief he carried in his pocket. Mrs Dobson disapproved of his using it for this purpose, particularly in company, and he avoided meeting her eyes.

'I've been contracted to search for a route to West Canterbury,' Arthur said.

Dobson had been told there was a Maori chief at Kaiapoi who might suggest a route, a dealer in greenstone.

'I went over the Alps last year as you know,' Haast said, 'but further south of course.'

After the prospector had got here first, Dobson thought. He heard Ettie opening cupboards to prepare the table.

'Doesn't it seem,' Mary said, 'as though West Canterbury is deliberately guarding its treasures?'

Dobson didn't bother to reply. He sensed that she was trying to be provocative.

'Many great risks are taken for greed's sake,' she said.

'You are greedy for us to pay attention, but you risk ridicule,' Haast said.

'Greedy or not, I'm hungry,' Dobson said. 'And it sounds as though Ettie's ready to serve in there.' They all rose.

Mrs Dobson said, 'Ring for the children, dear,' and Dobson picked up the dinner bell, to put an end to the dogs' fun.

• • •

'I reached a high valley, old glacier country, with a moraine – a gigantic heap of rocks, gravel, and clay – piled up at the far end. There was a sharp alpine bite to the air. Cold tarns spread across the valley floor – hebe, eyebright, and sundew crawled over the rocks.' Arthur must have added the botanical details recently, no doubt with Haast's input. The children listened with rapt attention to his account of the zigzag down, 500 metres into the headwaters of the mighty Otira Gorge, burying his boots in the scree for extra purchase. Haast was miraculously quiet, only nodding at intervals. While Mary expertly guided Heinrich's grabbing fist away from the dog's tail, Dobson saw the black beech forest dwarfed by altitude. He saw the geological drama unfolding at its own lumbering pace. He rigged imaginary dynamite blasts and planned pylons. The government had called him off the tunnel project to lead his own investigation into a road over the Alps. Since the gold rushes in West Canterbury had begun, the issue had become political, just as the Lyttelton tunnel had been in the previous election.

'I heard the banks might not insure coaches,' Arthur finally said.

'They might not,' Dobson said.

'And the freight will be far more expensive by the land route.'

'Until there's a railway it will.' At the prospect of pushing a railway through the Alps, they lapsed into silence. The less informed opinions being expressed in taverns and front rooms didn't interest Dobson much; nor did the agendas of the newspapers. He knew the road would go over Arthur's route. The best way to prove his point would be to build it. Schemes involving hot air balloons, or elevators powered by waterfalls, at least provided light relief.

Mary, too, was refreshing. 'How's your German coming along?' he asked.

'Do you know the dogs speak *sprechen Deutsch*?' she said.

'She tells them, "*sitz*",' Haast said. 'And calls it success when they understand.'

'And what do you think of this road, Mary?' Arthur asked. 'Are we all rabid for gold?'

'You might not be,' Mary said. 'But the government is.' Heinrich was reaching his hand out towards the dog's maw. Mary left him this time. 'They're used to it,' she said.

'They never snapped at any of you,' said Mrs Dobson.

The ageing dog, which had taken some time and trouble to achieve a comfortable position on its rug, flicked its head around and nipped at the ticklish fingers. The baby took in a silent, outraged breath while a tiny few beads of blood formed on the scrape. He was already being lifted by his mother's arms when he found his voice.

• • •

Dobson was tasked with building the road over Arthur's Pass. Conditions in the Alps were treacherous and his workers suffered. They died from disease, drowning, and rockfalls. Their fingers froze to their tools. In one fickle turn of weather, floodwaters washed away three bridges in the Otira Gorge. In the meantime passing diggers stopped to complain that the route wasn't ready. Six months into the project, roadmen carried Haast in his dogcart over the Bealey River. He continued on in his cart over the top of the pass, around Death's Head Corner, and down into Wright's Camp, becoming as he did so the first person to make the crossing on wheels.

Forty years later, when a power station had been built at the foot of the Devil's Punchbowl Falls and two new villages constructed for the purpose, work began on the Otira Tunnel, which would allow rail access from one coast to the other. It took fifteen years to complete. The tunnellers formed sports teams and raised families at either end.

Another seventy-five years on, Arthur's Pass would still be vulnerable to floods, landslides, rockfalls, and avalanches, and the government of the day would fund a viaduct across the Otira Valley, which would bypass the highest section of the existing road, home to Death's Head Corner. The Otira Viaduct would take two years to build. The extreme nature of the weather and landscape would make working conditions extremely difficult – for one man, fatal. The first cars would drive over in 1999.

The Bealey Hotel juts out on a spur where the Alps meet the Bealey River (for the Google Map, type 'Bealey Hotel, Bealey Spur, West Coast Road'). When the snow gets heavy and the pass closes, the Bealey is where the driver of the road grader is likely to settle in for the night.

DUCK PLUCK

The cement works at the Cape had an incredible view, as good a view as any similar facility in the world, but the workers' cottages, lining their own cliff-top cul-de-sac on the other side of the state highway, faced each other instead of looking out to sea. You could live an organised, unmuddled life on a street like that, Heather had always thought. She and her husband Rob lived in a far plusher new-build, ten kilometres away in town, but something about the uniformity of the workers' cottages appealed to her. They reminded her of the plastic houses in board games, identically square with pitched roofs and precise measures of lawn.

Rob had a thirty-year service record at the cement works when the plant was finally decommissioned. The company gave him first option to buy a cottage, so he and Heather decided to do so, and to rent it out as a holiday cabin. The cottages had been there so long – since the sixties – that, according to the painter-decorator, the fittings had become sought after. Sure enough, when the first paying guest followed Heather inside (her name was Raquel), she immediately said, 'Excuse me, but this wallpaper is amazing.' The beach nearest the cottages didn't have a name. To get to it, you walked back along the approach road, parallel to the state highway, passed the Good Mixer Tavern, then turned right towards the cliff edge. After a few homes and a football field the land stopped, and a path lined with gorse, spider nests, and cutty grass zigzagged downwards. When you negotiated the last steep section from the track onto the beachstones, frontwards if you were brave, backwards if you were nervous, and passed from one set of arms to another if you were an infant, the sudden backdrop of the cliff made it seem as though you had stepped off the island to potter at the edge of the sea.

If you were to continue straight past the Mixer instead of turning in, you would reach the lighthouse and the start of the seal colony track around to Addison's Bay. Addison's Bay was picnic-friendly. You could drive there and park beside the grass verge, which gave out onto a wide crescent of sand. Even at Addison's Bay, only skilled surfers would brave the waves, but there were rock pools deep enough for children to swim in, and smaller pools where they could disturb crabs and sea anemones. They weren't the attractively coloured anemones you saw on nature documentaries, but they at least closed on demand. The holiday homes at Addison's Bay were on the flat, so the families who stayed there could walk back and forth to the beach across the road. One such home, at the end of the row, nearest the heads and set back from the others, had recently been converted into a spruce café-restaurant that specialised in local seafood. The Dune Bar thrived on the business of blissed-out tourists.

'Erotic costume designer' was the phrase Raquel had used. She was American, and the term was probably American too. Heather wasn't sure what it meant. The American wanted some space, was what she said, but Heather couldn't help feeling that she had too much space, that she was isolated, so she stopped by the cottage with a feed of mussels one afternoon. She found her renter smoking on the porch. When she got as far as the front steps with the pail Raquel finally asked, 'Can I help?' She wore a large section of her shoulder-length hair swept across her face and pinned. The other side flared out to show a silver fan dangling from her ear.

'Hi. Just the door.' Heather followed her into the kitchen and lifted the mussels onto the Formica bench. Scattered across most surfaces were magazines and accessories: scuffed leather bags and finger-thick chains with charms hanging off them; Heather couldn't tell if they were belts or necklaces. There was a pile of dishes beside her laptop on the dining table.

Raquel picked up a plump shell from the top of the pile. 'They're so big. And inside?'

Heather held her thumb and forefinger a couple of inches apart.

'These are amazing.' Raquel lifted the pail by the handle and tipped its bottom to send the hoary shells rattling into the sink. 'The textures.' She put the pail down, went around to the table, and picked up a camera with a protruding lens, an SLR. Heather hadn't understood at first that this type of camera was digital. She'd assumed all digital cameras were like the one she and Rob had – slim, with automatic settings like Autumn Leaves, Fireworks, and Night Scene Portrait. Raquel grabbed the camera up with no more care than a child would a toy and pointed it down at the sink. Her side parting bulged and slipped forward, and she shoved the hairpin further in. 'There's so many. Where did they come from?' Her voice was slightly muffled by her hands.

'Off the reef, down the cape beach. The ban has just been lifted.'

Raquel pressed the button a few times. The camera made its reproduced clicking sound, and she dropped it to her side. 'Do people collect too many?'

'No, there's been an algal bloom. They're all right now, but they need a good scrub.' Where Raquel's fingers loosely gripped her camera, the crimson polish on her fingernails was absolutely smooth.

'I'll help you,' Heather said.

The landline at the cottage rang and rang. When Raquel finally picked up, there was a pause before she said 'Yes?' It would take them half an hour or so to walk around the heads to Addison's Bay, Heather explained, then another ten minutes to walk across to the Dune Bar, if they wanted to stop for coffee. Rob would pick them up.

Another pause. 'Sure, okay,' Raquel said. 'That would be nice.'

'I hope I didn't interrupt you in the middle of something,' Heather said. The sun was beating down. She should take an extra hat.

'No, I was just in bed,' Raquel said. It was at least noon.

The path around the headland dipped and climbed and turned corners through the gorse and flax. Heather stopped at one of the viewing platforms to point out the Towers, which jagged up half a kilometre off the Cape, and between them the Black Reef – you couldn't see the reef from shore, only the white wash where the waves broke against it. 'It was a sealing spot, way back,' Heather said. 'Horrible.' Raquel didn't respond. 'A French explorer named the Towers,' she said. 'd'Urville, his name was.' She didn't know if she'd pronounced it correctly.

'Oh yeah?' The wind flattened the hair against the back of Raquel's head.

In a hairpin bend, where the track turned down to the bay, was a signpost showing directions and distances. Most visitors – family of Rob's or friends from out of town – stopped there to find their city. They walked over like Raquel did, rested their hands on the rail (painted DOC-green, warmed by the sun), and gazed out over the Tasman. Past a certain point, of course, it was only a blue blur. Whatever they saw was only in their mind's eye. Raquel squinted up at the arrows, turned her head towards the States, and exhaled.

Heather had met Rob at the Good Mixer, not long after he started at the cement works. It was managed by a different couple then of course, that was 1970, but the pipe band passed through on New Year's Eve in those days, same as they do now – stood around in a large circle playing, just the same. At the beginning of every shooting season the Mixer hosted the duck pluck. Rob hadn't plucked the most ducks the night they met, but he'd come close, and he an outsider and not even off the land. The other competitors were all from families Heather knew. They mumbled, bringing their drinks to their mouths as though to cut themselves off before they could ramble past three or four sentences. Rob was extroverted and spoke out. When he got stuck into that pile of dead birds on the tarpaulin, the feathers flew. Married and at home, he became quieter, but she loved him by then. He'd strived to be solid, a solid person to raise a family with. Nowadays he took his own beer glass to barbecues. He had a particular type he liked to drink out of, a small stein with a handle. He enjoyed his sheepskin car-seat cover. He had reached a comfortable phase in his life.

The Dune Bar's deck looked out over an expanse of flowering flax to the bay itself, and beyond that the headland. The counter hand had drawn a koru in Heather's cappuccino foam. Raquel sipped a plain espresso and lit a cigarette. She was the only person smoking at any of the tables. 'A surfer's what?' she said.

'Squat. They stayed here without paying.'

'Oh okay, squat. That's an English thing.' She sipped away half of her espresso.

'How did you end up in New Zealand?' Heather said.

'I've been travelling for a while. Europe, Japan. I needed a creative break.'

'Creative how?'

'You know, for my work.'

Heather thought of photo-cards in foreign phone booths, magazines in the back rows of newsstands, and the annexes in DVD rental stores. 'They're all fakes,' Rob would say. 'Pumped up with God knows what.'

'I want to use more beautiful materials, get away from the zips and the PVC,' Raquel said.

Bondage. Suits during the day and punishment at night. Craven shuffling on all fours.

'It's not very inspiring around here,' Raquel said. 'You've got some farmers. That's about it.'

'So why did you choose to come?'

'I needed to be far away,' Raquel said.

'Away from what?'

'Who.'

'Pardon?'

'Away from who.' She blew her cigarette smoke off to one side and crushed the end into the ashtray. 'He's married.'

Rob chose that moment to clop out onto the deck. 'See any seals?'

Raquel waved a hand in front of her nose. 'Yeah, but we smelled them first.'

Heather thought Rob would meet her eye at this. He didn't like the kind of girls he called princesses – they weren't real women either. But he laughed. 'Gets a bit whiffy all right.' He swung his car keys around on one finger and caught them. 'Shall we stop by the Mixer on our way back?' he said. 'Toss the boss?'

You could see into the pub's back garden from a particular rise in the road, see the cross where the last dog had been buried, but from the car park all you could see was maroon-painted weatherboard and a high fence. Raquel had needed encouragement to get into the car, and she needed it to get out again: 'In you hop' and 'Out you hop'. When she finally made it into the open air she started walking towards the front door and Rob called her back. 'This way, love.' She fell into place behind him, headed for the side door the locals used. Following her, Heather noticed for the first time the asymmetrical cut of her black skirt and, when she turned back to check that Heather was still there, how heavily she emphasised her eyes with makeup. She'd smudged her eyeliner for the smoky look. When they got inside she eyed her new environment: the selection of peaked caps on the wall, from this or that construction firm or this or that beer brand; the money on the ceiling, the euros and greenbacks and yen.

The girl Cleary was at the leaner with a few of the Pollard boys, Heather could never remember which was which, and a couple of the other regulars, 4WD friends of her brother's. They would have noticed Raquel come in, but they took pains not to show it. Heather pulled a chair out for her at a table near the fire. 'We can play a game of pool if you like.'

'I don't know how,' Raquel said.

Rob was upbeat. It was happy hour after all. He put his hands on the table. 'What'll you ladies have to drink?' Heather said she'd have a beer with him, and Raquel asked for water.

'You want anything with that?' Rob raised his eyebrows

at Heather. 'Ice?' he said.

Raquel nodded quickly.

'Want to come up and toss the boss?' Rob said.

'You throw dice at the bar,' Heather said. 'If you throw higher than Tony, you get your drinks free.'

'Ah,' Raquel said, and didn't move.

'Maybe next time,' Heather said. Rob received her look and went off for the drinks. Bev was trying out a new karaoke machine in the corner, near the arch that led through to the eating area. She was singing 'Stand By Your Man' with the volume on low. No one was watching her. She had the lifetime tan of a surfer's moll. When Rob got back with the drinks, Raquel pushed her chair back and stood up.

'Sorry, I've got to go.' She walked straight out through the side door without faltering or looking back. She left her drink sitting there, a full glass.

'Too much ice?' Rob said. 'Not enough?'

The night was cool, the kind of autumn night that gives way to winter. When Rob got into bed he leaned over to kiss Heather instead of laying his head on the pillow. Sometimes he seemed to know better than she did whether she wanted to make love, but this time she'd been deliberate. She'd left the bedside lamp on and sat there propped up, not reading, not talking, until he'd lifted the covers on his side. They were some way into it, nearly naked and breathing each other's toothpaste, when a thought occurred to her. The lamp was still on, and she could see the fine wrinkles across Rob's eyelids. She closed her own eyes and summoned a mental image.

'Fuck me,' she said.

'What?'

She could sense him searching her expression. She clenched her eyes tighter.

'Fuck me,' she said. He laughed. She felt him pull away, and finally opened her eyes.

'Talk about your blindsides.' He drooped his head, clowning, and revealed his monkish bald circle. She realised then that she'd been ridiculous. That avenue was for the fake women of the world and their hairless, daintily scalloped genitals. She had opened the plain paper bag in his workbench drawer and seen the magazines there. It was a while before Rob had recovered well enough to continue.

• • •

The pakihi had been converted into farmland since the diggers had worked them over for gold, the iron pan broken down to allow for drainage, but some of the old ponds were still there – created when they built dams to feed water races, or formed out of the run-off from sluices. It was beside these ponds that the duck shooters set up their hides. Neither Rob nor Heather had ever been much for the shooting itself, but they had both won plucks since that first year they met. Most of the locals had at one time or another.

'Who's this?' Rob said, and pointed over with his eyes as he used the remote to chirrup the doors locked. Raquel was in a group of smokers at the side entrance with a cigarette sticking out from her hand like an extra finger. She waved the cigarette hand when she saw them. When they got up to the door, she gestured to Heather to lean in. 'Hey,' she whispered. She inclined her head very slightly to the side to indicate the man standing beside her. 'Paul's girlfriend has got a nurse's costume.' She smiled and pursed her lips at the same time, which Heather wouldn't have thought was possible.

'Come in and sit with us.' Heather thought the conversation with Paul had probably gone far enough.

Raquel flicked her cigarette out in front of her. It ricocheted off someone's bonnet. 'Okay, let's go.'

They nabbed some of the last seats, three stools at the leaner, and Rob went up for drinks. The front of the room was covered in tarpaulins, including the pool table, which had been pushed to one side. Another tarp had been draped over the ducks themselves, a waist-high mound. Tony was circulating with his clipboard. He approached a group of backpackers near the fire, three men. Raquel took a long sip of wine. 'Getting a bit colder now,' Heather said. 'I hope you've had the heater on.'

'Yeah, I've been hanging out in the cottage a lot. Online,' Raquel said. The pin that normally held her side part in place had fallen out, and she alternated between tossing her head and trying unsuccessfully to tuck it behind her ear. There was a pink film over the whites of her eyes.

'Are you feeling okay?' Heather said.

'She's getting to him. He's scared of losing the children.' Her pupils were different sizes. Portrayed like this, the wife had a touch of the shrew about her, the childhood sweetheart turned sour.

'Well he would be,' Heather said.

Tony had reached the front of the room. He began to

27

read the names of the male competitors off his clipboard, speaking into the karaoke mic.

'What exactly is going on here?' Raquel said.

'Just watch,' Heather said. 'You'll pick it up.'

The competitors each collected a rum and Coke from the rows set out on the pool table and sat down facing the rest of the bar. Up went Rob. Up went the stubbled backpackers.

'Where are you from?' Tony asked one, the tallest.

'Norway,' the man said, pointing to himself, 'and Denmark', pointing to his companions.

'An international field here tonight, folks,' Tony said. 'If you're new to this, think twist and rip. Twist and rip. And we're off.' The horn was always loud indoors. Raquel covered her hands with her ears, but too late.

The fizz was the worst part, Heather knew. If you were lucky, they'd had time to go flat. As each competitor finished his first drink, he reached out and grabbed a neck, wing, whatever he could get hold of underneath the tarp. A few men, including Rob, didn't bother placing their glasses on the floor. They swallowed the last gulp and dropped them. 'Oh my God!' Raquel said. Spectators had started yelling.

'C'mon Derek.'

'And another, Rob.'

The competitors tore out three or four handfuls of feathers per duck, the minimum they could get away with, and discarded them. After another minute the horn sounded for half time and the men ditched the ducks they were working on, tipped feathers out of their laps, and filed up for a drink. Heather counted the ducks on the floor.

Rob and the Norwegian had each finished four.

'Norway!' someone yelled.

The horn went off and Raquel cringed again. 'For fuck's sake.'

Heather watched Rob downing his second rum, slower this time. The Norwegian finished his in one go. The Danes were making a mess of their ducks, not tearing hard enough, pulling out only three or four feathers at a time. When the shouts of 'Norway' caught on, they began to watch their friend instead and only pull absentmindedly at the bodies in their hands. By this time the competitors were all sprouting feathers from the bunches of their sleeves and the rips in their jeans. Limp ducks, still fully feathered on the necks and wings but with their bodies exposed in fluff-tufted patches, swooned in heaps of three, four, five.

Rob was plucking his sixth. 'C'mon Rob!' Heather shouted. The Norwegian was keeping up with him. He threw his sixth aside and stood up for another. 'Who gets the feathers?' Raquel asked. Her glass was empty and she had a cigarette waiting between her fingers. Tony raised the horn. Raquel flinched. Rob flexed his hands and smiled as the judges stepped onto the tarpaulin.

Rob tipped Heather a wink when he rejoined her at the leaner – the rum and cokes must have helped to ease the defeat, she thought. 'Why does Raquel look like she hasn't slept for three days?' he asked her.

'Man trouble.'

'Did he chuck her, or what?'

'Sort of.'

Tony took his place beside the mound, which was now thigh-high. 'Ladies,' he said. The female competitors were pushing back chairs and passing their handbags to friends and husbands for safekeeping. 'Same rules. Same prize,' Tony said. The trophies waited at the far end of the pool table: two ducks represented in gold plastic, each on its own pseudo plinth.

Raquel made her way back to them. 'I can't understand what this guy's saying.' She'd brought an acrid tobacco smell back in with her. Tony began calling names and the first women walked over to collect their glasses. 'Most of these names I recognise, but there's one I don't,' he said. 'Where's Raquel?' Heather watched Raquel turn with the others to look around the room. 'Raquel?' Tony said.

Raquel frowned. 'No,' she said. Rob winked at Heather again. Raquel saw him. 'No no no no no no no,' she said.

Paul, whose girlfriend owned a nurse's costume, pointed from one of the tables. 'There she is!'

'No way.' Raquel brought a hand up beside her face, but Tony had spotted her. 'Come on up, Raquel. Dark horse over there took the men's event.'

Head still lowered, she twisted around to where Tony was pointing. The Norwegian at the fireplace smiled an alpine smile and raised his eyebrows. She turned her head back, lifted it just enough to look into Heather's eyes, then pushed herself off the leaner. 'Okay, I have a question,' she said.

The spectators all watched her make her way around the chairs up to Tony in her high-waisted jeans. When she arrived, she tucked the sweep of hair away from her face and it fell forward again. She leaned into the mic. 'My question is, if I do this, can I have the feathers?' The hum dampened. Heather hoped she wouldn't explain.

30

'Tell you what, love – we've had plenty of people ask if they can take ducks home, but never the feathers.' Tony opened his palms towards his mates at one of the tables near the front, the shooters who had brought the ducks in. Eventually they nodded.

'That's a yes, love,' Tony said. Somebody howled like a werewolf.

'All right I'll do it.' Raquel looked down and side-stepped away from something she saw poking out from under the tarpaulin. 'No way, this is fucking disgusting.' There were cheers when she swore. They all watched her descend from the height of her heels into one of the school chairs.

Something was detaining Tony behind the bar: a keg needed changing or a pipe had come loose from the dishwasher. 'I'm not going to just sit here,' Heather said. She slipped off her stool. When Tony looked up and saw her weaving between the tables he picked the mic up from beside the bottles of sprits. 'A last-minute entry, ladies and gents. Quite an event we have on our hands.' He lowered it, then remembered something and raised it again. 'Collect your drinks, ladies.' He put the mic down and bent under the bar while Heather lined up with the others to get a drink. She took a seat beside Raquel. Three of the waiting women leaned in to chat, and another waved to someone at a table. Raquel put her glass on the floor, picked up a wing feather and ran her fingernail through the barbs, watching them separate and flick back.

'That's plenty of time to brace yourselves. Let's get amongst it. I've said it before and I'll say it again – twist and rip, ladies. Three, two . . . ' he raised the horn, 'one!'

The blare filled Heather's head. She took a couple of quick gulps and lowered her glass. The fizz burned the back of her throat. She gulped again then breathed. Syrupy sweetness rushed in with the oxygen. She tipped her head back for one more gulp. And done. When she stepped forward and reached under the tarp to drag a duck away by its feet, Raquel was only just retrieving her full glass from the floor.

'Get into it Heather!' That was Rob.

Heather had always plucked her ducks in much the same way that she drank the rum, mechanically. But as she took the duck into her hands now she understood that she had a certain expertise. The technique came back to her with the weight and feel. Clutching the tougher exterior feathers she felt the familiar resistance, then the giving way. The old competitiveness rushed back. She tore out another fistful and dropped her first duck.

Reaching forward to pick up her second bird around the middle – the tarp had deflated to around knee height – she allowed herself a glance sideways. Raquel's empty glass was lying beside her chair. She was gripping a bird around the neck with one hand and had the other hand held open. A few feathers had stuck to her palm. She was looking down at the bare patch she'd made, at the duck's sad, dimpled chest. Her hair covered half of her face.

'It's easier if you hold it by its feet,' Heather said.

Raquel looked up in surprise.

'No fraternising, ladies,' Tony called.

Still surprised, as though she was watching what somebody else was doing, Raquel grasped the legs and let the neck go.

32

The Norwegian, Kristian, joined them. Theirs was the champions' table. 'I'll tell you what,' Heather said. 'If there was a trophy for the single best-plucked duck, Raquel would have taken it home. You were fastidious about removing those feathers.'

'What are you going to do with these?' Kristian asked. Raquel had a rubbish bag full of feathers parked up on either side of her stool.

'Wash them,' she said.

'And then?'

'I don't know. Do you think birds are sexy?'

'Sexy? Birds? No.'

'Me either really. I don't know. Maybe I'll stuff a pillow.'

Kristian raised his glass. 'Skål.' He eyeballed each of them in turn.

Heather picked up her drink to follow his lead. There was a proper way to do these things. 'Skål.' She sought out Rob's gaze and held it.

THE SINNER

Drunk, but not quite crazy, on most days Laurence proclaimed old news and damnation from his upturned beer barrel, ten paces along from the doorway of Greene's Provision Store. The wide dirt street grazed a riverbank, like the famed Left Bank of Paris and Thames Embankment did, but was usually almost empty. This was the town's main street, the Strand. Near the corner of the Strand and Prince Street, a newsmonger could reach his public. 'Quicksilver!' Laurence would yell, two weeks late. 'Shipment of quicksilver. Find out where to buy it.' Or 'Fenian rising! Massacre in Cabul!' Most of the time Laurence couldn't remember the future he had originally imagined for himself. Now, his plan changed from day to day.

Greybeards were rare and represented old-time expertise, so newcomers courted Laurence with drink. He took it and told them to go home, to find wage work on farms or building churches. Some days he gestured at violence, prophesied doom. Diggers threw him coins out of superstition, to ward off his soothsaying. He sat in a funk of bad air and bad humour, amid rumours of crime, desertion, and love. Badly healed blisters mottled the skin across the ridge of his cheeks. Past him, back and forth, speculators would walk and talk mining stock. They disappeared into the Empire Hotel to seal their sales with whisky. They passed in and out of the broker's office and the warden's court. Before they had the machinery to crush the gold from quartz, before a church had been built or even a bank, they were trading.

Duncan met up with Bill on the shingle that trailed into the river, and they made a foray into the bush to find a route over the alps to the east coast. They helped each other across roaring creek-beds. They climbed, slipping on moss and grabbing at pungas, to a height where they could sink a stripped branch into the soil and tie a pilfered linen tea cloth onto it. Exploring on a grander scale, Duncan thought, crossing real alps and cutting tracks, would require the same skills, only more time and extra equipment.

Bill sank the stick into the ground and Duncan tied the tea cloth onto it. Bill, who lived at the Empire, had been boasting that his father kept a pistol under his bed. 'He hired four dancing girls as well,' Bill said.

Duncan broke off another branch tip, which made a high-pitched crack, and grubbed in the leaf bed with it. 'What are their names?'

'Annie, Kate, Barbara and Lou,' Bill said. 'I can mesmerise them.'

'Can not,' said Duncan.

'Look,' said Bill. He folded his front lip under with the side of his index finger and rubbed the finger back and forth against the gum. When he took it away his lip stayed where it was, leaving his gum exposed so he looked like some throwback. Duncan used his stick to support the spine of a young fern frond.

'My father has quicksilver in the shop. I drank some.'

'Did not, you damn bastard.'

They slipped back down the slope, soil streaked with greywacke, calling each other bastards. They balanced on the same rocks again to cross the creek, just a trickle of a creek now, still calling each other bastards. And they called each other bastards for the rest of the walk back to the shingle bed beside the Strand, where they parted for home. 'I have a word for you in my mind,' Bill said, stepping backwards. 'It starts with B.'

'Your mother called you Bastard. Bill is your dancing name,' Duncan said.

Black tea and potatoes on the table in the kitchen attached to the back of the provisions store. Plain scones. 'God bless this food to our bodies,' said Duncan's mother. Duncan was especially familiar with this posture: the crown of her head, the dark hair scraped aside from her scalp, the looming knot of her bun. 'Amen.'

Two thumps on the back door seemed to respond.

'For God's sake,' Greene said.

Duncan's mother excused herself and scooped the curtain aside.

'Needs his neck pulled.'

They heard her footfalls, the wooden scrape of a plank drawn out of a bracket, and the rattling of the swollen door until it struck the frame at the right angle and slipped out.

'The papers got here.'

When Mrs Greene opened the door to the yard, to the darkening charcoal and pearl in the sky overhead and the ruts in the mud leading out through the gap in the fence, Laurence was there, meditating on a large delivery crate. Small victories were all he asked for – small improvements and small finds. 'I don't think the day was given to us for laundering,' she said. This was her habit, to behave as though they were only passing time.

'Do you think God is laundering?' Laurence said.

'If so this should be a very clean place.' She sought to save him the embarrassment of asking. 'Mr Moss, would you say that crate was heavy?'

'This? No, I wouldn't say so.'

She frowned down at it. 'Firewood, according to my husband. But it's always damp, sitting outdoors.'

'Doesn't look very heavy, damp or not.' He jammed his reading matter under one arm and with the other he dragged the crate from the shop's yard and tipped it sideways on the Strand. He established himself inside it with his neck jutting forward, eyeing the shop doorway. 'Skittle alley,' he told the street, 'opened in Brighton.' The clouds were gathering to rain. A few leaning bodies passed, like low clouds blown along the street.

Duncan stepped out onto the front porch of the store. Keeping a wary eye on Laurence from under a hat that was too big for him, he held the copies of the latest edition ready in a fan. 'Little Grey discovery. It's a big one,' he said. Laurence began to yell. Duncan tried to ignore him and sidestepped a few paces. 'Papers here. New gold discovered,' he said. The clouds let go.

Laurence was hollering directly at him now. 'Increase your noise! You have to shout!'

A pair of diggers approached. Raindrops pelted the timber roof of Laurence's crate and clattered on the corrugated iron awning outside the store. Duncan looked up at the men's beards and at the picks hanging off their backs then down at the coins going into his palm as the folded leaves of newsprint slipped out of his hands. The rain drew a curtain around the awning and the diggers waited in the dry. Their swag rolls resembled horse collars slung across their bodies. The man nearest to Duncan had words stitched into the bottom edge of his blanket. SACRAMENTO SAM. It wasn't elegant, like initials embroidered on a handkerchief. He'd used brown wool, and the strokes of the letters didn't match up.

'Excuse me, how long is the track to the Little Grey?'

'Why, you lighting out?'

'Beg pardon?'

'Are. You. Running. A-way?' He said it as though he were talking to an imbecile. He laughed, and his mate laughed.

'I want to tramp to my uncle at Totara Flat.'

The American pointed. 'Couple of good hours from here out to the bottom of the saddle. That's where we head tonight. Then a gutbusting climb tomorrow.'

'Damn,' Duncan said. He twanged it slightly.

Sam's mate smiled and turned a page over. 'Damn is right.'

They kept arriving – speculators, camp followers, diggers. They helped themselves from the pile behind Duncan in the doorway and showered coins that fell around his feet and were stamped into mud, and he wouldn't have the correct amount later, when he scooped them out of his pouch to hand them over behind the counter, at rib height to his father, who, if he was in the right mood, when Duncan tried to explain would bang the heel of his hand at half-strength into the side of Duncan's head. All comers stopped at Greene's to buy their supplies of flour, bacon, and tobacco. Duncan listened to them arguing routes, discussing the state of the river crossings and the topography of the Little Grey.

Diggers drained out of the creeks that fed into the Inangahua River. A number crossed on the punt at the Landing. Others undressed and forded the river from the Strand, hefting their swags over their heads, water breaking around them. They tramped across Fern Flat towards the saddle, pans flashing in the late sun, and pushed into the bush path: dragging sluices on sledge, wheeling handcarts, and sitting up on horseback. At intervals the trees opened out and the sun reached Duncan, throwing his shadow across the track into the rust-coloured undergrowth. He kept Sacramento Sam and his mates in view. In an hour or two he would offer to carry the riffle board that jutted awkwardly from the bundle on Sam's back. Duncan's mother always shook her head at the men she saw spilling out of the hotels. 'Forgive us our sins,' she'd say. Because she did, Duncan associated sinning with the beery stink of the Empire Hotel and with Bill's pig-hunting father. He aimed to be a sinner. He invented the first line of a song, walking the route west to the Little Grey Valley in the last of the daylight. *Duncan was a sinner and a wealthy man.* He had heard of boys aged thirteen or fourteen who worked on gold claims. He was twelve.

• • •

Sacramento Sam was travelling with two mates. The man at the front introduced himself as Sam Lord. He whistled on-again-off-again, calling to birds, immersed in some memory, or thinking of entertaining the others. Duncan didn't know why he did it, only that it was irritating, especially when he stopped in what seemed like the middle of a line, stayed silent until he seemed to have finished, and then started again. Roots jutted up and tripped Duncan's boots. Rays leeched in through the canopy and needled his eyes. The heavy wingbeat of a wood pigeon bent a bough in one of the beeches just off the track, and Duncan watched Sam Lord reach an arm back, grip the butt of his rifle, and slide it out from his bed roll. He had paused again, mid-melody. Distracted, Duncan walked into the flat bottom of the iron pan tied onto Sacramento's swag, staggered back and sideways with the extra weight on his back, and made a frustrated growling noise inherited from his father – at that very moment it entered his vocal repertoire. As he did, he heard the report of the rifle. 'Damn it,' Sam Lord said. Sacramento waited for Duncan to regain his feet and lifted up his billy, a third full of slopping water. It had a metallic tang, like melted gravel.

Soon after they started again, Sam Lord half turned his head so Sacramento would hear. 'They chased the police out of Goldsborough a few weeks ago.'

Sacramento's pannikin and billy rattled together with each step. 'I heard they sent constables over from Christchurch posed as diggers,' he said.

The other mate, behind Duncan, spoke over his head. 'What can they find out anyway, 'less they see you. What name do you know me by?'

The men in front didn't reply.

'What is your name?' Duncan asked.

'Sam,' he said. 'I'm Irish Sam, so if you want me to answer, you call me Irish. Hey, what's my name?' he shouted over Duncan's head.

'Irish,' Sam Lord shouted back.

'And what do you know about me? About my past?' Irish said.

'You're Irish,' Sam Lord said. They looked to Duncan like landlocked pirates, moleskins stuffed into the tops of their boots and knives hanging off their belts.

'That's right,' Irish said. 'Try policing that.'

Duncan vaguely knew he couldn't sleep there, upright on a mound of tussock, but he wanted to try. 'Fetch some wood. This stuff, dry as you can,' Sacramento said. Under the tree cover at the edge of the flat, most of the loose branches had rotted. They made a wet crunch as the fibres broke apart. Even dead, the supplejack vines wouldn't snap cleanly. When Duncan dumped his first armful of slimy

41

brushwood, Sacramento was mixing a paste. When he got back with his second, there were flames popping through the kindling. Sacramento used a stick to lift the lid off the billy and scooped spoonfuls of tea into the steaming water. The fire was pouring smoke, chasing the damp out. 'Go and put your gear in the tent,' he said.

'I haven't got one.'

'You're in with me. On the left.'

Duncan turned to face the tents and stuck his thumb out to make an L. Inside, he spread the ferns that Sacramento had left for him, rolled his mat out, and put his folded blanket on top. He wanted to lie down but he could smell the damper, and the lid of the billy was chattering, so he picked up his pannikin and took it back to the fire and stood looking into the flames as though his limbs had forgotten how to fold.

'You'd better sit,' Sam said.

Murmuring reached them from the other parties on the flat – groups of four or five, same as theirs, their tents flapping open and snapping in and out when the sou'easterly flowed through a channel between the peaks, passing around and between them, fanning the hottest embers to a creaking peach, lifting the soft white ash, tipping the flames sideways and sending smoke into the men's eyes until they thought better of their positions and shifted. The earthy rot released by the warmth of the sun had died down. There were only localised aromas from their pots and the private staleness from each man's body – behind that, clean air. The wind lifted the scents and carried them off.

Irish rinsed his mug out, tipped a few dollops of whisky

into it, and passed the bottle to Sam Lord, who took some and passed it to Sacramento, who took a measure, put the bottle down beside him, and poured tea into Duncan's outheld cup. 'You wanna see something?' Irish said. A gobbet of bacon fat had lodged in his beard, just below his lip.

'No,' Sam Lord said. Sacramento opened his book.

Irish bunched his undershirt up over his stomach to reveal the peak-shaped depression between his ribs. He looked down at himself. 'See that?' he said. Sacramento, head bent over his book, moved only his eyes to look.

Duncan couldn't see anything, then he could just make out a darker patch like a round shadow at the apex where the ribs joined. He looked at Sacramento. He looked back at Irish. 'What is it?'

'Ever heard of a third nipple before?'

The nub was only half-formed.

'We've had animals with abnormalities like that, if we bred them too close,' Sam Lord said.

Irish pulled his shirt down. 'Here, see what you think of that.' He handed his mug to Duncan.

Duncan narrowed his eyes in anticipation and tipped the mug up. He let the spirit flood his mouth, and gulped once. He let it flood his mouth again until he felt it knocking against his gullet – this was all the liquid in the cup – and swallowed again. He stiffened and focussed on quelling the impulse to cough. His eyes filled.

Irish was letting in and out a kind of wheeze that served for a laugh. He took his mug back, looked into it, and held his hand out for the bottle. 'Was worth it to see that,' he said.

From reclining on his side Sam Lord sat up, his nose glowing with sunburn. 'Righto,' he said. 'I have a party trick.'

'No, wait. I've got one,' Duncan said.

Sacramento shifted his book on his knee. 'Drink your tea,' he said.

'It might not look right.' Duncan folded his top lip under and used his index finger to push it up away from his teeth. He rubbed his gum back and forth with the side of his finger to dry the moisture off. 'How's that?' he asked, taking his finger away. When he spoke he moved his mouth as little as possible to keep the lip where it was.

'Another inbred,' Sam Lord said.

'Who taught you that?' Sacramento said.

Duncan ran his tongue over his gums to wet them again. 'My friend Bill.'

'And that? Where'd you get that?' Sam Lord said. He was pointing to the back of his own neck.

At first Duncan didn't understand, then he lifted his hand up and rubbed at his bruises. 'My father,' he said. Sam Lord nodded. Irish drank.

Sacramento closed his book. 'Anything you get at home will be nothing on what could happen to you out here.'

He hoisted his swag over his head and jigged it up and down on his knotted shoulder. They tramped over to the start of the track, where someone had erected a sign, charcoal on a splintered panel, To The Gold.

A stand of kowhai spilled over the flat, blinking yellow, ruffled by the wind. Wood pigeons filled the low boughs like baubles. Sam Lord slid his rifle from his swag. 'Keep still until I go,' he said.

They descended into the Little Grey Valley from the north. Duncan's skin felt infused with a residual heat, but the temperature was falling away. Birdcalls – fluid piping, squeaking, and kissing – lacquered the treetops.

Kamahi Camp was deserted. They crossed the flattened grass, kicking mounds of ash and middens. They saw only one man. The fire outside his tent sputtered scraps of smoke. As Duncan watched he crawled out, stabbed at the embers, threw another stick on, then crawled backwards and flopped down again, his head and shoulders still outdoors.

The few buildings clustered on Kamahi Flat, where Old Man's Creek met the Little Grey, didn't have a name yet. Gordon's, they were calling them, after the first publican to build there. His saloon resembled a railway platform and station house. Boot soles clobbered the planks of the veranda. Duncan sat sucking from a glass of sarsaparilla on a bench against a wall, looking into a stand of slouch hats and beards, moleskins and serge. The *Grey River Argus* was to blame, so they said – publishing spittle from a drunkard's lips. Variations on the story accumulated along with the new arrivals, new details and theories thrown in. A veteran prospector had put the news out during a drinking spree at Twelve Mile. Accounts of what he shouted at the bar and what he promised in the creeks ranged widely. A case of Champagne, some said. A whisky fountain, said others. Nuggets like knuckles. The creeks had duffered out in six days – a handful of parties were making change from tucker, but they wouldn't support more. The diggers mourned the claims they'd left behind, channels they'd cut that would already have collapsed, sluices too large to transport.

Somebody had walked away from a sweet deal: tucker and three pounds per week working a coal seam.

Somebody had a girl waiting in Dunedin.

One man hadn't eaten anything but potatoes for five days.

One man said he could slice the lips off the lying clown's face. He'd have another drink, and he'd go downriver and lift him up by his neck.

He had all the coal he could burn and a hut.

He boiled them and ate them green and all. His guts were scoured dry.

Grace. Her name crossed the air between them like an imported scent.

The public house opposite was flat-fronted, kept its doors closed and was lit inside with lamps, even during the day. But people tended not to drink there during the day. It faced Gordon's across a strip of earth that was only a street as far as those two buildings could be said to form one. The proprietor had painted a proper name on a sign, but it was known as Dooley's. Gordon's had a veranda and looked out across the valley. Dooley's had two barmaids. Dooley had lured them from Melbourne by describing a gold town-cum-seaside resort. He met them off the boat at Hokitika, which was not so far from what they had in mind, and loaded their suitcases onto his dray for a one-day journey north and then a further two days upriver.

Duncan sat on another bench, cushioned this time, drinking another glass of sarsaparilla. Sam Lord and Irish were watching the barmaid from a table nearby. Sam Lord was sketching her. She reminded Duncan of a doll off the top of a music box, except he'd never seen one of those serving drinks. She turned towards him and walked out from behind the bar, smiling. 'Is one of these your father?' she said. Duncan stayed silent, considering. She sank onto the bench. He was eye level with her neck, bejewelled and frilly. Her hair flowed – it was loose at least, he could see where it ended – and in the caress of the gaslight it seemed soft.

'You're feeling sleepy,' he said. She looked out to the room. What? her eyes asked. Sam Lord, who was closest to Duncan at the end of the table, mumbled something to Irish. 'Very sleepy,' Duncan said. The woman's eyes, a troubled grey, said, Anyone? Can anyone tell me what this is about?

'Sleepy so you can't think.'

Her eyes eventually came back to him, so far from obedient that they bleached the intentions from his mind. 'All right, Mr Lullaby. Give's a shilling and I'll show you,' she said. Irish wheezed. Sam Lord flicked a shilling into the air towards Duncan, who reached up and clapped it between his hands too loudly. Dooley looked up from his table in the corner. The woman reached over from her nest of skirts, took hold of each of Duncan's two middle fingers with two of her own, and peeled them apart to reveal the coin sitting on the shell of his palm. He watched her pick it up. Later in life he'd abandon a woman for being less uppish than this. 'I'm leaving. Pack my bags,' he'd say; but just then he languished under what he assumed was some kind of witchery.

The barmaid rose up, and in a baffling flight of fabric she enveloped him in her skirts. He was inside a cage of petticoats, pressed against her chemise. Her stockings sagged into the tops of her boots. Light leaked weakly through the layers of fabric. He was trapped in a cave of lavender fumes and something else, below that. 'I can't breathe,' he said to her chemise. He thought he heard more laughter.

The barmaid looked down over the tiers of fabric at her new legs, scrawny and facing the wrong way. She stared out into the room, and her eyes asked, Did the sun come up from the west today? Is the Earth inside out? Will I wake up soon in a cottage in Antrim, at the hearth with my mother?

One by one the tents went dark. Duncan cowled his blanket around his head and listened to the rain on the canvas in the sour humidity. His bundle of belongings topped off with a hat made the shape of a slumped drunkard, like Laurence on the Strand at the end of a hot day.

Outside, he heard the men get back. 'I say we look up the creeks,' Sacramento said. 'Damn this knot. Who tied this?'

'You did. You're on a hiding to nothing up here,' Irish said. 'There are thirty parties up those creeks sifting yesterday's shit.'

'I'm going up the Little Grey tomorrow. Sam Lord?'

'You know payable ground that way?'

'I have some idea of where to look.'

'All right.'

'What happens to the boy? He needs to get to his uncle.'

'There's no uncle in Totara Flat.'

'He said he was in the post office.'

'There's no post office on Totara Flat.' Sacramento said. 'Boy's no obligation of ours.'

'Go to hell then.'

'Is this not it?'

Duncan thought of his room at the back of the store in town and of the kitchen, where the stove was always lit. He had been five when it came upriver on the punt, dragged behind two horses then lifted by his father and three other men up the steps and through the kitchen door. He didn't realise he had been asleep until he heard the rain. But the sound was off. The rain was hitting something in front of their tent, wasn't falling true. He watched as the flap lifted open and Irish leaned in. 'Boy. Duncan. You awake?'

The foot traffic was all downriver. Spotting rain accumulated on the brim of Duncan's hat and dripped in front of his eyes. He had the air of a dejected bootblack or pickpocket. They'd find a claim to work, Irish told him. They tramped the riverside track while water soaked into their clothes. When they reached Totara Flat, where the track improved, a carter offered them a spot. They sat on the planks with their legs dangling. The going was slow, and the ruts and rocks jarred their tailbones. The carter turned to shout back to them off and on. He was glad to have company, he said. 'You come from that mess up the valley? Not much joy up there.'

'Not much,' Irish shouted.

'Not a good day for you and your boy to travel.'

Irish put his hand on Duncan's shoulder. 'He's used to it.'

'Where are you headed?'

'To see my uncle in Greymouth,' Duncan yelled.

'And what's your name, son?'

'Sam,' Duncan yelled.

• • •

In his shack behind the Empire, Laurence lit a lamp and rested it on a pile of curling newspapers. He snipped a twelve-inch length of wire in two. Using his pliers, he bent each section into a scrawled pair of legs. He passed a longer section through a barrel stopper prepared as a body and twisted the surplus up into a neck, bent it forward and threaded it through a smaller cork for a head. The length sticking out from the back of the stopper curved over to make an upstanding tail. His fingers were more flora than fauna, but deft.

New rain crashed onto the loosening shingles above his head while he squinted to attach the front and back legs. The dog entire was the size of his hand, but it wasn't the size that gave it personality; it was the prominent chest, the legs stout and wide-spaced, and the high tail. This was a yapping rat-catcher. When he put it down to get a better look there were two, one made of wire and cast-offs and the other a flat black copy on the wall. He lined them all up: the weka, the fat publican, the dancing girl, and the others. Their shadows trouped across the back wall. He thought as he often did of giving them to the shop boy. He wondered whether the boy might be too old for toys, then he remembered again that he had gone.

ADMAN

Justin was setting a new display ad for Saturday's edition – Wrigleys were having a special on leaf blowers. He had the feeling he often got on Fridays, a fusion of tension and potential. Especially this Friday. He was building up to a big weekend. That night, first up, a leaving do for someone from work. The next day, his father's fiftieth. The birthday party was a big deal. People were arriving from out of town. His mother had been cooking all week and his father had painted the fence. Justin was supposed to have mowed the lawns.

Lunchtime. He left work and walked away from the port inland, towards the hills. The clouds were spreading and joining up. On its own block between the service station and the motor lodge was the old cinema site, empty and graded. All gone, the lobby, popcorn fountain, ice-cream bar, and ticket booth. Thank you for not smoking in this cinema. *Intermission*. Down to the right of the screen, the side door's EXIT sign glowing green.

Theirs was the house with the neat front lawn and a Masport parked up in front of the garage. His father was in the kitchen holding a tin of shoe polish. 'Who finished the lawns?' Justin asked.

'Your mother.'

'Where is she?'

'Gone to buy wine.' There were already supermarket bags on the bench waiting to be unpacked. September, the *National Geographic* calendar said – a photograph of a blue hole in Belize. 'What time's your work thing tonight?'

'Bus leaves at seven. What's in the tin?'

'Piss off. Bring us back a paper.' His father pulled the back door shut behind him. Justin opened the cake tin and took a piece of apricot slice, a kind of spongy orange sandwich.

Back at work, afternoon. He could hear the deep blat of a motorbike idling at the intersection. Probably a guy off the fishing boats straddling his Triumph. ('Someone must have hacked into my phone.') Inside, the printery technician was arguing with his service provider. ('I live alone.') One of Justin's ears popped for no apparent reason and whistled faintly, then faded out. ('My mother stays with me, but it wouldn't have been her.') He took one of the mandarins Deb was offering around in a netting bag. ('She's 83!') Deb had been friends with his sister since they were kids. ('Do you have notes about this? I spoke to one of you yesterday.') In Justin's mind, she wore lace in pale colours – pink, powder blue, and peppermint. On his first day, when she'd leaned forward to pick up his induction pack from a pile on the front desk, he'd been able to see the hang of her breasts down the front of her top. ('Doesn't it come up on your screen?') It wasn't so much the breasts themselves but the dark hollow that had taken the edge off. ('021 323 4999.') In the quieter moments of that day his thoughts had curled up and rested there. ('0-2-1. 3-2-3. 4-9-9-9.') So yes, he'd take a mandarin if she offered one.

At home again that evening. His newer jeans on and wax rubbed into his hair. Justin shook the hands offered to him by his father's friends. Firm grips and quips about his aftershave, the chain loop on his jeans. He picked up a mini-samosa from a plate and broke it between his molars, breathing the steam out. There was no sunset, only a grey void, getting darker. The lounge lights were beginning to reflect in the windows. 'Tell you what I read recently,' his father started.

'Here we go.'

'When gibbons mate, they do it five hundred times in two days.' They suddenly got loud when they laughed.

'Where'd you get that from?'

'This – birthday present from work.'

'Give's a look.' One of the cronies took the book from him (front cover a solid block of red; title in a scrawly font, yellow) and started reading animal facts aloud. Justin's father picked the remote up to mute the news. The sound it made tapping back down on the coffee table was as familiar to Justin as his sister's footfalls in the hall. That was the coffee table she and her friends had used for séances.

'What about you Justin? Out on the prowl tonight?'

'Maybe. Anyone know any good pick-up lines?'

'How about "It'll have to be your place cause I live with my parents"?'

He hadn't realised what they were doing at first. He'd walked out of a movie that night, a backwoods slasher. He'd been restless. He had a Friday feeling then, too, like a full-moon instinct, only weekly. He'd crouched outside the lounge window to gain a visual at half-past nine or so, in the last of the light. The gauzy net curtains had helped to conceal him. There were four: his sister, Deb, and two others. For a makeshift Ouija, they'd laid Scrabble letters out on the coffee table in an oval, with a Y and an N at either end.

He skidded in his socks through the kitchen to the dining area, around the corner from where the girls were kneeling.

His sister was using her class-rep voice. 'Can you see us all the time, including when we're alone?' There was a pause then a scrape as the glass began its traverse. 'Y,' the class rep announced, to wondering murmurs.

'How can we test him?'

'Ask him a question only one of us could know the answer to, then that person should take their finger off the glass.' His sister again, using her noodle, aged fifteen.

'Someone ask it what colour knickers you're wearing.' These girls were insane.

'Wait, let me check,' Deb said. Only a few metres across the carpet, she was pulling her jeans away from her hip and peering down into the gap. 'Okay.'

His sister took over again. 'So what colour is Deb's underwear?' Justin waited for their spirit visitor to use its x-ray vision. The glass started to move again. This time it didn't stop but picked up speed, skating in circles, faster and faster, building up momentum until it suddenly stopped mid-circuit.

'Whoa.'

'Where is it?'

'What letter was it?'

'The M. I've got it.' In the slasher version, this would be the moment when they heard the first noise outside.

'M for what, mauve?'

He saw them, high-cut, filled out, but Deb must have shaken her head.

One by one, between swoops around the board, punctuated by the occasional stutter of glass on rimu, their voices recited the letters U, R, and D. After D there was a ringing clatter as the glass tipped over, and someone – it was his sister – said, 'Oh my God, murder!' It would have been her pushing the glass all along. 'Someone killed him.'

'Whoa,' Deb said. 'Ask him how.'

Back at work to catch the bus. WEST COAST NEWS EST. 1869. Under his strides the road seal glistened in the street lights. Tyres hissed past. He climbed the steps and bumped fists with the driver. The guy whose leaving do it was, a reporter, was at the front, passing cans back from a carton at his feet. He held one up and Justin stopped. The engine rumbled under them. Aussie dollar was strong, dude – money to be made. Had Justin thought about going? Deb was in an aisle seat halfway down. Oblivious to Justin, she plucked the cotton of her top between her thumb and index finger and released it to bounce off some crumbs. She left her fingernails natural these days. When she'd got bored in class she'd coloured them in with a Vivid, or painted them with Twink. She'd sketched the same thing over and over again on her ring binders, a line drawing of a female face with a cross-hatched tear on the cheek.

'You have to be persistent. That's the secret to dealing with the big telecoms. In the end they'll pay to get you off their backs.' Justin was listening to the guy from the printery when Deb called him over. He slapped the top of the guy's seat to excuse himself and moved down the aisle. As the driver guided them out onto the road he landed in the empty seat opposite her.

He saw Deb at work all the time, but she seemed more distant from him than she had been at school. ('Your Dad's birthday thing is tomorrow night, eh?') She'd got better at controlling her personality. ('Yeah.') He'd stood in the hallway outside his sister's bedroom door the night of the séance ('Is sis staying at your folks' place?') and listened to them squealing, hyped on violence. ('She is, yep.') Eventually he'd pressed his ear to the door, as though trying to hear her heartbeat through her cotton-clad chest. ('How are they?') The muffling of their words only made him more curious. What were they laughing about? Why were their voices moving around? Before he'd had time to pull back properly, the door to his parents' bedroom had opened and his father had stood there in his pyjama bottoms, squinting. ('They're good, Dad's started the party already.') That had been a Friday then and this was a Friday now. Tomorrow, his sister would monopolise Deb's time. His father's friends would take the piss. They'd all be watching. It had to be tonight.

FLOOD

Constable O'Brien arrived unannounced at a camp in the Grey Valley. Steady rain had accompanied his five-hour ride from Nobles, and his horse moved forward with its head lowered. The rivers were already only a sporting dive from bridges, and punt crossings had all but halted. When the diggers caught sight of O'Brien, shouts of 'Joe' went up from multiple directions. 'I advise moving these tents tonight,' he called out above them, and the cries tapered off. 'The river will continue to rise.' The water moved behind him with the authority of gathering mass. 'Is there an agent selling supplies here?' he asked. The digger nearest to the legs of O'Brien's horse pointed to a raised terrace behind the camp. O'Brien thought he would visit hell itself for a position in front of a good fire.

Back in Greymouth, the Inspector had handed O'Brien the lists of claim disputes and grog licenses. 'Anyone who resists your enquiries, be the Ahab to his whale.' The Inspector wore the same style of three-button waistcoat and dangling pocket watch as George Dobson had been wearing when they recovered his body not far from the Arnold River, the year before. The killers had buried the surveyor with his Inverness Cape spread across his legs and his compass and field book lying on his chest, as though to help him navigate the next world. The Egyptians had sometimes buried their dead with model boats, such as O'Brien's son would enjoy. O'Brien felt his love for his children as a kind of discomfort. It caved his chest with feeling to see their slick shoulders rounded over the waterline in the bathtub.

By the time O'Brien had tied his horse and left it tolerating the rain, the agent had ducked under the tent flaps to greet him. 'Robert Cooper,' he said.

'O'Brien.' If O'Brien were called upon to identify Cooper, he supposed he would do it by the thin stature and the green sash tied around his hat. It wasn't often he saw a storekeeper so slight of build. *I identify the body by the hands, the teeth, the colour of the hair, and the way in which he wore it*: the words of Dobson's brother-in-law. Beyond Cooper, O'Brien could see two figures in the tent and hear their voices. One was that of a woman; whether she was a lady he couldn't tell. 'See your license please.'

The man inside the tent raised his voice to reach them. 'A form of punishment, is it?'

O'Brien spoke to the canvas. 'Sorry?'

'Sending you out during a big wet.'

Cooper lifted a flap up to let him through. 'Come in

and sit.' O'Brien knew the man who was seated there, and gave the name time to stir. He was identifiable by his height and the right angles that made him up. His brow hung like a bluff over his eyes. A dog, sporting breed, sat between his crease-worn boots, its chin glued to his knee. Then he remembered – it was the prospector George 'Moonlight' Fairweather. The diggers followed him around if they could find him. O'Brien would tell his son about this meeting.

'Don't stand,' O'Brien said, though Fairweather hadn't moved. The dog hadn't as much as lifted its chin.

'George Fairweather.'

'Yes.' O'Brien reached over and shook his hand.

'Miss Ellen Cooper,' the woman said. She was dressed respectably but not for practicality. Her gloves were lace and her skirts, draping to the ground, were hemmed in three inches of mud. O'Brien had a sense that he should know her as well. 'Actress,' she said. Apparently she expected him to know her. Then he remembered that he did – knew *of* her, at least. Miss Ellen Cooper of the Prince of Wales Theatre. Juliet with round arms.

'Hello, Miss.'

Cooper put an extra chair down. O'Brien sat and scanned his license. 'Are you related?' he said.

'She's my stepsister,' Cooper said.

'So you're one of the Coopers in Greymouth? I hadn't thought,' O'Brien said, then he regretted commenting on what he had or hadn't thought in relation to her.

'Have you seen me in a play, Constable?'

'This is in order.' O'Brien passed the licence back to Cooper.

There was random incidental timing, such as looking

down from a coach at the moment a boy spits, seeing the saliva in midair. Then there was the kind of timing that might change something – Fate, according to the classical Greeks and Romans. Despite Dobson's being young when he was killed, something like twenty-five years old, there had been evidence of old injuries, bones protruding in his hands and long-healed scars.

'You haven't said whether you're being punished,' Fairweather said. He seemed touched by the stage himself in his breeches and boots. Cooper showed O'Brien a bottle and O'Brien waved a hand in refusal.

'I don't know about that,' he said, with regards to the punishment, 'but I do know, or I'm fairly sure, that river is going to burst its banks tomorrow.'

This prompted an outburst from Miss Cooper. 'I haven't had time to learn my lines, helping Robert, and now I don't suppose the coach will be able to get through, and I was hoping to learn them on the trip. Ten o'clock in the morning tomorrow, the driver said.' Her eyes landed on O'Brien, then Fairweather, and finally her brother. 'Rehearsals start tomorrow night.'

'Even if you do make it out tomorrow, they won't hold any rehearsal.' Cooper shifted in his seat. 'And even if you do make it out and they do hold one, you won't be given permission to go.'

Nights like this in locations like this, it was hard to credit that not twenty miles away lamps were burning in the streets, pianos were being played, and wine was falling into fine crystal. O'Brien's children would be eating – half past five sharp – and his wife would be tending their manners. Slipping a fork out from between a thumb and forefinger and turning it over. Brushing an elbow off the table. His bones told him to accept the whisky and stay where he was, but O'Brien knew that apathy could be as good as self-slaughter. 'You might be called on to feed the diggers in camp if you get cut off,' he said.

'I'm authorised to extend credit,' Cooper said.

Rumour had it George Moonlight was never harassed, even if he was more likely than not to be carrying gold.

'Do you mean to ride back tonight yourself?' Cooper said. 'Will the river allow it?'

'I'll try for Greymouth tonight,' O'Brien said.

Miss Cooper raised her head. 'Could anybody –'

'Will you hush?' Cooper said.

O'Brien had Red Jacks, Twelve Mile Creek, the Arnold, and Stillwater to negotiate. The bridge at the Arnold was solid, but it hadn't yet been tested in floodwaters like these. Last July he had searched along the western side of that river, guided by a description one of the killers had given. When they finally found it, Dobson's body was lying in boggy ground. A phantom of the stench had transferred itself to O'Brien. On his arrival home he'd seen distaste flit across his wife's face. In the children's abandoned bathwater, he had scrubbed his skin, soaped his hair, and used a stick under his fingernails. 'I'll have a drink after all,' he said.

'That cook in Hokitika was hanged, I read,' said Cooper. 'And he deserved it.'

Miss Cooper widened her eyes and blinked. In her plays, the dead rose again to take bows. Not yet two months earlier at Squaretown, O'Brien had seen a mob of diggers tie a pickpocket to the wheel of a dray, crop his hair and beard, and take turns at kicking him. O'Brien had stayed quiet for fear of harm against himself. He was one against a hundred. 'He at least got a fair trial,' he said, meaning the cook. 'They resort to harsh methods on the new fields.' He had always used the phrase 'harsh methods' to refer to such violence.

'It was worse in Victoria, and worse again in California before that,' Moonlight said. The disorder grew worse the further back one cared to look – scalpings, bodies dangling from roof beams – stretching all the way back into legend. There was a reason religions made use of gold, O'Brien thought. It attracted the eye to a virtuous path. The only gold in their house was around his wife's ring finger. But he had also stood by and watched a trail accumulate on the mats across a collection table. He also understood the unique satisfaction of that.

Above their heads the canvas sagged around the centre post. The fire flickered up bravely at the entrance. O'Brien accepted a second pour to strengthen his resolve. The air was so damp he was breathing moisture into his lungs. Cooper had a fey cross of the legs, he thought, for all his pretended authority. 'What brings you to camp, Miss Cooper?' O'Brien said. Fairweather refused a second whisky.

A look passed between Cooper and the girl. She was cradling a glass of sherry. 'I'm here because my father is a Philistine,' she said.

Cooper shook his head. 'She was carrying around a letter written to her by an actor.'

'He was a forbidding Lord Montague,' the girl said.

Fairweather said, 'So it's her who's being punished.'

O'Brien saw a devious blusterhead slipping her notes at the back of an echoing hall, perhaps even bundling her up behind a curtain and grasping her plump arms, kissing her cheek. He didn't find it amusing.

'I observed that the flesh was wanting on the side of the left cheek,' the Inspector had written in his report on the Dobson recovery. 'In lifting it, almost the entire skin of one hand fell off like a glove.' They had finally found Dobson's body at the end of a timber-felling track. The Inspector had recorded the details of the scene then put Dobson's compass and field book aside and supervised while O'Brien and the Special Constable lifted the body onto a stretcher. They packed soil around the face and shifted the cape to lie over the head for the boat trip out. One man had admitted to striking the blows that were evidenced in the inquest, and another to causing the marks around the throat. None of the gang had confessed to laying the cape over his legs as though to stave off a chill. For most of his life O'Brien had assumed that there was a higher power directing events, but in the past year or so he hadn't been able to discern any intent, only blind moments following one upon the other.

The colour of the sherry had been taken up by Miss Cooper's complexion. As O'Brien swallowed the last of his glass, she spoke. 'Constable, would you take me with you to town?'

'You hardly deserve it,' Cooper said.

'I don't mind about the rehearsal now,' Miss Cooper said. 'I just want to be back in town with Ma and Pa.' The firelight shone in her eyes as though reflected in water.

Cooper gave in. 'Our father would rather she were in town if the river is going to flood.'

O'Brien thought they might make it as far as Red Jack's before the first difficult crossing. They might have to spend the night there. 'Yes, I think I could take her,' he said. 'There are safe places to stop downriver if we get stuck.' O'Brien swallowed the last of his glass. He cleared his throat and tried to push back against the complacency brought on by the whisky. He didn't feel inclined to battle against whatever design or happenstance had put this girl in front of him. If the universe could be indiscriminate, why shouldn't he?

'The three of us could travel together,' Fairweather said, looking down at his hands on his thighs. 'Three's better than two, crossing a river.' Miss Cooper was visibly relieved, convinced now of her escape. O'Brien felt as though he had been lifted and held floating for a moment before being dropped again.

Cooper nodded at the supplies. 'If I wouldn't be leaving all of this behind – I appreciate the favour. It's well known you prefer to keep your own timetable, Mr Fairweather.'

'These are special circumstances,' Fairweather said.

The scene outside hadn't changed greatly – a river plain dulled by clouds, perhaps duller still. The diggers had uprooted their tents from the riverside camp and humped past now with the bundles. Thunder rolled out of the gullies. Only two hours remained of the present gloom that passed for daylight. Cooper helped his sister up to the stirrup by making a hammock with his hand. When she had settled herself behind Fairweather – his was the larger horse – her lace gloves slipped around his waist. There was nothing else for her to hold on to. Her cape spilled down either side of the saddle and blended them together.

Caused by whatever clash of giants, whatever despaired sobbing of gods; for whatever means of punishment, destruction, or pursuit, the downpours and snowmelts of spring sent water plummeting off the mountainsides and into the creeks and tributaries of the Grey. Diggers awoke being lifted towards the ridges of their tents. They clutched on to their swags to stay afloat. They climbed trees and clambered up slopes. The flotsam started small, with scraps of brushwood, grip poles, and spades. White water became full-bodied and heavy. The river scaled its banks, no longer containable. Bodies floated: bovine, canine, and equine. Even human – crossing Stillwater, O'Brien was able to reach into the current and grab hold of a boy's body by the collar. He guided it around, laid it across his horse's back, and carried it out. To his surprise, when they reached the bank and the horse propelled them up onto dry land, the boy began coughing.

Down the Grey came demolished bridges, camps, and tramlines. O'Brien's group approached the outskirts of Greymouth while floodwaters rushed trunks along the waterfront, sloshed through shops, and fanned out to encroach on backstreets. Set in against the hills, men smoked on corners and women carried food between houses. Their streets sloped down then disappeared underwater. Fairweather and O'Brien put Miss Cooper in the first boat that would have her and waited for another.

O'Brien watched her conveyed across the water, a triangle in her cape. He took the flask that Fairweather handed to him. In what had been solid grey overhead, clouds began to take on shape and outline, to admit the possibility of clearing. For the final two miles on horseback, the two men had been compiling lists to pass the time, and they continued out of exhausted habit. They listed execution methods: firing squad, stoning, crucifixion, drawing and quartering, beheading, impalement. The boy suggested walking the plank, and they allowed it.

THE KITCHEN PIG
SMOKES THE
MOUSEKETEERS

When I arrive, Brynn is in conversation with a hygiene inspector. He sends me out to his car for the laundered tablecloths. The guy doesn't look like food safety somehow, and the extra car I see outside doesn't fit either, an eighties Falcon. I put my ear up to the lid of the boot, but I can't hear anyone tied up in there. Colliding with him in the hall I ask, 'Is I arrested, officer? Do you need to use your handcuffs on me?' His hairdo I would describe as respectable, and on his feet he wears the open-toed sandals favoured by bushwalkers.

'I don't know what you want, but I'm finished here.'

I do a bit more inquiring, Cam-styley. 'Have you got a badge, food policeman?'

'That's funny.'

'You don't, do you? You just have that sad little brochure.' I point to the reading matter he brought with him, but a satisfactory response ain't forthcoming.

'Cam! Where are you?' This word-making is coming from the vittles station.

'Bye bye Germ Fighter.' I blow him a big bacterial kiss. To the man in the kitchen: 'Coming!'

I go in to Brynn and put the question. 'Is our food in danger?' The man's jeans are riding low on his hips.

'We have to rearrange the big fridge. Pass me three lettuces,' he says.

'Lettuces: one, two, and trois.'

'Not so hard. Tomatoes?'

'Tomatoes.' I pitch the bag over to him, but the tomatoes all misbehave in mid-air and come spilling out of the neck when he tries to catch it. 'Ho. Sorry.'

'No throwing, just passing,' he says.

'Sorry. I got excited.'

'Celery.'

'Scalpel.'

'Radishes.'

'Suction.'

'You're an idiot,' he says.

'I know you are. You said you are. But what am I?'

He leans to look out through the service window. 'Shit, that's the rafting trip. Go on then.' Ladies and gentlemen, a vanload of triumphant tourists with wet underwear, fresh from dien raftpaddlement.

I give Terry the list of wet consumables, a power tune playing in my head. *Eye of the tiger, it's the cream of the fight.* A paddler has followed me up to the bar to look at the whiskies, so I point in the right direction. He's Jameson's, all the way.

'Jameson's please.' Hot damn.

Terry, to him, 'Good choice.' To me, 'Wait there, Cam. I'll pour the rest of these now.' *And the last known survivor –* the paddler points at my bodice, asks me.

'Picked it up at a costume sale.' He's a seventies fan right here. What comes after *And the last known survivor*? The not knowing is an itch on my brain. Paddler points at the tray, asks me.

'This? I can carry this with my arms tied behind my back. Go and sit down.' *Bam, bam bam bam, bam bam bam, bam bam bam . . .*

Terry regards my frontage, crease-browed. 'Jesus Cam, haven't they been scared enough?' I had very few clean garments to don for dinner service, so I have on my Wonder Woman costume. I haven't hit them with the starry supershorts, though, just the bodice and the headband. My jeans are all-conventional.

'Do you want me to change?'

'Forget it. There's too much to do.'

'Is Annabelle coming in?' If his young wife don't want to start early, she don't start early.

'At half past. These drinks are ready to go.'

Risin' up, back on the street. One tray full o' liquid lovin', comin' atcha.

In your blocks. Wait for my signal: three, two, and one. They're off and racing! Who do we have in lane one, Cam? In lane one, Cam, is an American couple who drove from Nelson today – suspiciously even tans, possible naturists. And lane two? Starting at two we have four trampers fresh off the Paparoas. You can expect disorientation and

70

gratitude from them this evening. Moving across the field now, you'll see the staff of the *West Coast News*. They're out for a leaving do in lane three. They'll be pissed as buggery in no time at all. Holy Cam, who's this? Retirees travelling by campervan on a tight budget? Give them a thrill. Put them in the snug. And where do we think Her Royal Breastness might be hiding at this minute? Is she at home getting a few voddies on? Flicking her bean? Shooting at tin cans with a miniature pistol? There's the ting of the food bell. I perambulate to the service window. 'Table two plating up – two groper first. What did Terry say?' Brynn asks.

'She'll be here at half past. Watch out for a cake on the second shelf.'

'When did we start a BYO food policy?'

'Birthday girl.'

'Go. You're coming back for a tortellini and a shanks.'

Even our habitually unruffled leader has an air of being perturbed when the salon-bronzed gorgon still hasn't appeared at half past. He gazes at the phone. The rambunctious members of a to-do list are tapping their feet and clearing their throats in my head space, but even in this distracted state, I'm struck by a prediction. In the current customer-heavy climate, we are going to lose our barman to a rescue operation. 'I'm worried, Cam. Could you phone Tim?'

'Kayaking.'

'Emma?'

'At her Nan's seventieth. You know, she's not officially missing until tomorrow evening, and a zillion percent of people show up in the first 48 hours.'

71

'One hour. Then I'm going to find her.'

For the next hour I go into hyperdrive. Useful superpowers might include mind-reading, telekinesis, and a savant's talent for addition. Instead I have two mortal hands and a paper and pen. Main courses for the newspaper coming up next. Clear table two, the weary mountain toilers. They'll want dessert, huzzah. Replenish drinks for blue-haired Bonnie and corpulent Clyde over here, the campervan renegades. And what do you know? Another hungry couple has just walked in with a squirming she-devil, and table five is open like the gap between her front teeth. Terry seats them and gives them a high chair for their twister, menus, water. I leave my drinks order on the bar, and there's the bell for the *News* mains. I slide their steak knives to them across the table. I'm at the window and Brynn pins the order up.

'Steaks first. Burned to blue, left to right. Veg stacks are next.'

Time strikes nine. Still no troll. Terry is gnawing on his nails. He has shrunk three sizes. 'Go,' I tell him. I put bills down, weighted with mints, for the American couple and the hikers – two direct hits – and take coffee orders on the birthday table. Sweep for used plates on my way back to light the candles. The Kitchen Pig has taken off his smeary smock and tied a black apron around his waist. I give him the coffee list and lift the cake out of the fridge. The picture is a ninja princess and the words are Happy 10th Birthday Amber! Turn down the stereo, dim the lights; carry the glowing confection across the floor with a stage inhalation, 'Haa–' in you come, that's it, don't leave my jaw gaping here '–aapy birthday to you.' The birthday table joins in, plus the campervanners and a good handful from the *News*. The birthday girl is taking the attention well. The polish on her fingernails says princess, but she's 100 percent warrior when she takes down the candles. I go back for the side plates. The Paparoas posse have laid their notes in the tray. 'Reallygood,' they tell me, 'thankyou.' Pushing those gaps between words is just too much effort sometimes. Pick up the tray. Brynn hits the bell to tell me the latecomers' pasta is up. Dingding.

A majestic downpour, gratuitous rain. The back door is open and a breeze pushes through. Monuments of dinner plates teeter on the bench. Bread baskets have spilled their crumbs over the floor, and knives and forks lie where they fell trying to reach the cutlery baskets. Brynn is elbow deep in dish gore. I show him the cakestand. A ten-year-old wiseacre has remoulded a fistful of yellow sponge into a cake shape and stabbed a candle in the top. 'Hungry?'

'Not for the rest of my life,' he says. He takes his apron off. 'Drink?' We push out through the double doors, in the manner of cowboys in spaghetti westerns. A hombre from the *News* is last at the bar and brings us in on a factoid he's telling to a chiquita in glittery pantyhose.

'I read somewhere that pound for pound the Jack Russell terrier is the most vicious of all animals.'

'What about ferrets?' says his muchacha. 'Ferrets are nasty.'

'Ferrets are dawdlers,' Brynn tells them in a monotone. 'Never know when to leave.' I'm hunched over the bar. Don't look to us for entertainment, amigos.

'Bored. Let's get out of here,' says the leftover. While she steadies herself on her heels, the kitchen doors swing open to let Terry through. He veers off to the side somewhat in his approach.

'Annabelle's left me,' he says. The Kitchen Pig lets the register slam open.

'She left a note,' Terry says. 'Apparently she wants to find herself.'

'I wouldn't wait up if I were you.'

'Cam.' Brynn gives me a look. 'Did she say where she was going?'

'Do either of you have anything to smoke?' Terry asks. I'd like to help him, even if I do call this a lucky escape. I find my pouch in my bag and roll while he talks. 'She's been seeing this prick from a youth rescue centre in Greymouth.'

'Do you know him?' Brynn says.

'Don't have the Coaster credentials. Cam might know the family.'

I pass over the joint and give them my best Corleone, stroke my chin: 'Family? I don't get mixed up in Family business.' I wait for a reprimand, but Terry is smiling, leaking smoke through his teeth.

'Cam is what happens when a person watches too many movies,' Brynn says. He sucks on the joint and passes it to me.

'Weird thing is,' says Terry, 'in her letter she said the guy has been here. Said he got a sample of the "negative energy" she's been putting up with.'

'Negative energy?' I say. I come over all sci-fi. I'm thinking black holes and imagining getting sucked into

74

one, which isn't a predicament that lends itself to merritude. With THC orbiting in my circulatory system, it's of the utmost importance that I pull myself back out. 'Whaddaya say we take this outside?'

They achieve the required gathering of belongings, space jackets and such forth, in slow motion. I'm feeling insecure. There are astral journeys between us. We need intergalactic interpreters. 'Oh wait, the rain,' I say.

'Rain's stopped,' says Brynn. And it has. All we can hear is pot clanks from the kitchen and the swish-hum of the dish machine. We exit through the swing doors and collect the Kitchen Pig on our way through. He snuffles his gratitude. He grunts his thanks. He mumbles, I suppose I should say. The heavens have closed but we opt for the awning anyway, where the picnic table is dry. Brynn lights the patio heater and the four of us line up, not on the seats but on the table. We breathe our fill of fresh air then pass the joint again and light new cigarettes.

I'm going somewhere with a ditty about the people in your neighbourhood, from one of the Jim Henson shows. 'There was a grocer right? And a doctor?'

Brynn is stuck on a tennis player he idolised. 'I used to pause the video player and imitate his serve.'

'I saw that guy on some shopping channel selling a watch,' I say.

'I wanted to be just like him. I even wore the same sweat-band.'

'The Mickey Mouse club! *M–i–c . . . see you real soon . . .* ' I sing the song.

The Kitchen Pig makes a gun with his hand and picks off the mouseketeers.

Chewing the chat is enjoyable, but the stars are shining above us to conjure distance and black holes.

'Well,' says Terry, 'I guess that's that then.'

'What's what when?' says the Kitchen Pig. He's genuinely asking, and it takes our addled brains a few seconds to register what he said. We all start laughing and it takes us a while to stop.

'Yeah, that about sums Annabelle up,' Terry says. He wipes the back of his hand across his eyes.

'It wasn't that funny,' the Kitchen Pig says.

TOUGH

The Morning Star Race collected water from a creek above the Kaniere River and spanned six miles of swamp, bush, and lumpy paddocks – tree cemeteries with stumps for headstones – to supply the gold claims on Kaniere Terrace. The flume reared 60 feet skyward above Tucker Flat for half a mile. The same timber they had logged from the flat formed the support poles and struts. On the terrace itself, the main flume dropped its liquid cargo into a gigantic overshot wheel, which fed the tailraces that branched out to individual claims, allowing operators to wash the earth they dug across their tables and send the mullock into a sludge channel flowing across the base of the terrace.

Not long before the race was christened, the founding pair of the Burgess Gang had been among the Kaniere claimholders, lying low. They aimed to convince an adversary of theirs, a lawman, of their honest intentions. For six weeks they worked the claim before turning back to their chosen vocation, staging a series of robberies during Christmas time in gold country. Their first targets were lone prospectors. In the early months of '66 they doubled their numbers. The four members of the Burgess gang could claim between them past lives in prize fighting, hotel keeping, and gold trading. They limped up the West Coast in a poorly planned crime spree. They were evicted from Hokitika. They were evicted from Greymouth, but not before they had murdered a surveyor they drunkenly mistook for a gold buyer. The gold buyer himself travelled with a disguised police escort. By the time they finally located him, the foursome had become more discerning. Lying in ambush, they recognised the escort for what it was and refrained from sticking the party up. Their journey north continued. When they arrived in Westport to rob the bank, they learned that it had closed down.

The gang finally caught up with their destined infamy near the summit of the Maungatapu track, east of Nelson. They crouched behind a rock, waiting for a party of diggers they knew to be carrying money and gold. Spread before them was a lush, mountainous view.

When they made their getaway they left behind a derelict house in charred ruins. There were scraps of clothing mixed in with the embers. They left behind a packhorse they had shot in the head and left to slide down a bank. It eventually came to rest in the scrub at the bottom of the gully. But this wasn't desecration enough: when they returned to Nelson they had also left behind five human victims. They kept hold of their loot for four days.

Tough was working the tables on Kaniere Terrace, where it had all begun, for a party of brothers from the English Midlands. He had shared in the early excitement kicked up by the Burgess gang; they too could compete with the crimes of the original Wild West. Those bushrangers knew what they wanted and they went after it. Tough had to give them that. The trick was to have a specific goal. He himself was making a good wage, but money wasn't enough. It had to be combined with panache or audacity. Around the time of the Maungatapu murders, a bush fever seized Tough's guts and scattered his wits. He suffered loose, bloody stools and loose, bloody thoughts for four days before seeking medical help.

Kaniere township was bisected by the flume of the Morning Star Race and punctuated by waterwheels. Its theatre called itself the Paris Opera, and its barbers called themselves professors. The man Tough sought out had earned the title of doctor by placing an advertisement in the local gazette and by possessing a medical chest, which lay open, beyond reproach, on his desk, lined with velvet and hugging glass-stoppered bottles in individual compartments. The good doctor's most prized piece of equipment, featured prominently in his advertisement, was the Davis Kidder Magneto Machine. When he had settled Tough in the patient's chair, he placed the brass electrodes of this machine in Tough's hands and cranked the handle to generate a flow of electricity. Almost immediately, Tough wanted to let go. When he did, he couldn't detect any immediate improvement in his condition, and nor would he; the vagaries of biology were hardly likely to reveal themselves to someone like Tough.

Feverish and pained, Tough tried to focus on the objects in front of him while the doctor washed his hands in a basin behind the desk. Laid out in the drawer of the mahogany chest were a bone-handled scalpel, an ear horn, and a set of ivory teeth. The doctor's trousers stretched around a rotund stomach. He gazed out of the window. 'Considering the circumstances, we can blame vapours,' he said. 'Dampness, rotting wood, decomposing vegetation . . .' It seemed as though he would continue indefinitely in the same cheerless tone, inspired by what he saw, but eventually he turned around to face his desk and Tough sitting on the other side of it. 'Harmful gases from the atmosphere.' Tough worked out in the open, but vapours could travel, he supposed, and in any case he wasn't likely to argue with a man who had a bone saw hanging from a nail knocked into his wall. The doctor mixed a tincture by scooping a fingernail of carbolic powder from its bottle and tipping it into a glass of sherry from a decanter, which resembled the medicine bottles in the chest in every aspect except its dimensions. 'Has anything aroused strong passions in you recently? A conflict or a tragic circumstance?' The doctor placed the fizzing glass in front of Tough.

'Not that I can remember,' Tough said, and picked up the glass.

The doctor recommended that Tough refrain from physical labour for at least two weeks to aid his recovery, but that he take clean air for half an hour every day. Tough didn't dare stray far, so he took to pacing the rows of tents at camp every morning. The various parties tended to bunch together: the Germans in rows one and two, the Scots at the far end, and the Irish in the middle. His reconnoitres of the far reaches of the miners' quarters soon earned Tough suspicion from the camp warden, who reminded him to stay on the designated pathways rather than cut between tents, lest he disturb the guide ropes, or so the warden said.

Tough amended his route to lap the camp entire. With the doctor's diagnosis in mind, he stayed out of the bush that bordered two sides of the encampment. He kept the trees on one side of him and the tents on the other. His stomach could cramp at any moment, though, so his new route was a comfort to him, even if he did risk a sickening lungful of plant miasma. So it happened that he stepped off the perimeter track late one morning. He was half concealed, taking shallow breaths, behind the bushiest fuchsia he had been able to find in the time available to him. He'd at least finished and pulled up his trousers, but was still buttoning his fly and smarting with vulnerability when the warden's voice startled him. 'Ahoy! Who's there?' (The warden had spent a year as a cadet with the Royal Navy off Portsmouth.)

'Yes?' It was no good, he couldn't make the deft movements under pressure.

'What are you doing in there?'

'Am I now prohibited from standing behind a tree?'

Lingering fever or none, Tough had resolved that morning to find somewhere he could recuperate without feeling scrutinised or judged. He joined the poker table at the Commercial Hotel. In the mornings, he would leave the camp and trudge the mile to the township, past the creak and swing of the Pioneer Wheel and past the bunched two-up school, busy with betting, that operated in the hotel's side yard during the day. The Spinner would flip the coins out of the kip up, up for ten feet or more, and Tough would push the hotel door open.

Most of the players were hunched and drawn. Those who had recently crossed the Alps from East Canterbury sported lumps of skin on their lips. Sunburn on their cheeks, noses, and foreheads lent them an air of manic health. Tough played against men whom fortune had favoured and those it had deserted. Who would speak up and tell an anecdote? Who would laugh the loudest? The man who neither told anecdotes nor laughed at them was the poker face to reckon with. Tough played and won. He fed on curried beef and doughboys. His mind, for some time rippling and billowing with fever, came gently to rest. If it settled around a few wrinkles, then what mind hadn't?

Well into his second week of playing, Tough felt confident enough to bluff on a pair of fours. It was mid-afternoon, and none of the players had yet displayed any swagger. When it came time to slide his coins into the pot, however, a muscle in the top of his cheek, just under his eye, gave a spasm. He blinked and opened his eyes wide and shook his head, but the muscle continued to jump at intervals of five or ten seconds. The players saw the hand out, but Tough's tic had unsettled the others. They voted unanimously to see his hand on the first bet, and he lost to a middling two pairs – threes and nines.

This was the first appearance of what would become a debilitating handicap for Tough. Every time he tried to bet on anything less than a pair of aces, his cheek would begin to twitch. The other players soon learned to read him. With only luck to rely on, the last of Tough's funds soon leaked away. When they did, a matter of two weeks after the visit to the doctor, his place on the terrace claim had been filled. The pre-fever Tough would have been affronted. Post-fever Tough was relieved – not for him the inch-wise shovelling of gravels for another man's gain.

For regular money and revitalising wafts of coastal air, ferrying coaches across the Nile River seemed a good occupation. If the spring rain hampered Tough's efforts on the river occasionally (there was nothing peculiar about spring rain; rain could be counted on whatever the season, but this happened to be spring), then the sparkling face the earth showed to the sky afterwards, the powered-up colour, guileless greens and blues, and the water itself, its transparent skin plumped smooth, soon earned his forgiveness. The local bush – surely it couldn't ever have caused him harm – shined from every leaf. He passed the time of day with the drivers of the postal and the passenger coaches, who puffed on their pipes while the punt swung out and Tough eased it along the guide ropes on the current. He wasn't staying in camp any more but in his own shack of beech planks, set back from the riverbank and comfortable in the new season like a breathing body.

He and his assistant were on the water one dawn replacing a damaged rail when Tough felt the gentle but unyielding impact of what he at first assumed were logs carried downriver in the spring floods. He was prying the splintered rail free, keeping his eye on the nail as he felt it begin to slide out of its timber bed, and he didn't look up right away. His assistant, carrying the new rail from the bank, did, and let the length fall out of his hands. That was when Tough raised his head and saw the bodies of two diggers. They rose and dipped with the water, jostling against the punt at different angles: one had cartwheeled to make impact head first, and the other had pulled up alongside as if seeking to berth there. Both men's eyeballs were gone. Submersion had turned the tissue in the sockets white, and they were filling with river grit. The haphazard angles of the corpses and the movement of the water underneath animated them in a way that sent Tough stepping off his punt for what would be the last time and hastening up the path towards his shack, leaving his assistant to report the deaths; to catch the men's belts and collars with a boat hook from the bank, to check their pockets, and to wait with them until the next coach arrived.

When Tough departed for Nelson, the members of the Burgess Gang were going to trial there for the murders at Maungatapu. People had always said that the northern climate was more hospitable, dry and sunny, but this public event gave the town an extra allure for Tough. He hoped to attend. On his first day of travelling, he followed the tramline towards Cape Foulwind. Bush robins bounced on branches beside him and grubbed in his footsteps. There was a toll for walking the tramways, so when he heard a piano accordion and a singing voice, he stepped off the tracks amongst the scrub and rotting logs, and waited, mulch underfoot and hillocks of cloud in the blue overhead. He heard the steady timber scrape of the car on the rails. He saw the horses first. Heads dipping, foot-heavy, they carted their load at a pace that wasn't much faster than Tough could walk. He crouched, breathing the warm ferns, hoping the colour of his skin wouldn't stand out between the fronds and flax spears. He didn't see the tram's final approach. He waited while the tune became clear enough to recognise, 'Lady Mine', then the car was upon him all at once. He could have run alongside, reached out, and snatched the hat from the singer, who had taken it off his head and held it dangling out the window.

Later in the day, Tough sat on his swag above Eel Creek to smoke. Contorted trunks leaned out from the undulating limestone. Picking a sour piece of tobacco off his tongue, he watched through the leaves the shapes of two men below him climbing the gully track. He didn't hear them speak. They passed out of sight for the last section, then emerged twenty paces ahead, turned and started back towards him. He saw then that they were wearing something over their heads – masks or cloth. It was too late for him to conceal himself. At ten paces, he could make out the lettering on the white-and-blue cotton flour bags that covered the men's heads and bunched at their shoulders.

When they met on the track, the larger of the men said, 'Sandflies,' and lifted his bag to reveal an ordinary friendly face. 'Vicious on the river beach.' Tough held his hand out. The man introduced himself as Jim Donoghue and his companion as Li Chen. Li Chen didn't speak. 'How you off for tobacco?' Jim said. Tough handed over his pouch. Li Chen didn't meet Tough's eye through his holes, and shook his head when Tough took the pouch back from Jim and held it out to him. 'Quiet sort,' Jim said, striking his match against his belt. He hooked the bag up over his nose so he could smoke his cigarette.

Over the lip of the bank then, another man pushed out through the bush onto the tracks. His head, too, was covered, but in a coarse hessian sack. The man's body spelled out some degree of surprise as it straightened, his head turning between Jim and Li Chen in their flour bags, then he lifted a pistol and pointed it at them. 'Down, get down,' he growled. The three of them clambered down between the rails, Tough and Jim side by side and Li Chen opposite. Tough heard the clacks and yoohoos of birds in the bush and watched the man's boots step towards them and disappear, and he heard the dulled thump of boot against body. Jim groaned. 'Empty it. Everything you've got.' The boots crossed diagonally to Li Chen and one of them tilted his body a few inches off the ground.

Tough felt no admiration, only a panicked paralysis, limited in focus to the corduroyed track immediately under his nose. A sandfly landed on the rail in front of his face. He didn't dare move. While the two other men wormed their hands into their shirts, Tough jerked his chin up. He saw Li Chen deposit two leather bags on the ground in front of him. The assailant lifted them slowly, distracted by rapture. Each bag hung, the contents pulling the leather tight. Tough had never seen so much gold belonging to one man. This was the dream, the homeward bounder, and they were going to be killed for it. The highwayman wasn't going to roll them a cigarette, tell them a joke, or kiss anyone's hand. He was going to shoot them like lame horses and the birds would start calling again within the minute. Tough heard Jim stir beside him, a dragging of cloth. Li Chen tucked his head back down.

'Relinquish your firearm! Police!' Jim shouted. The attacker lifted his head and his weapon together and Tough flinched from a blast beside his ear. The moment played itself out at high velocity, robbed of effect in the isolation. Tough kept his face pressed to the ground, waiting for the world to right itself. The go-getter, who for a brief moment had held in his hands a haul that was worthy of a police escort, bent and tipped over between Tough and Li Chen. He lay face down as though he were studying minutiae on the ground. The man took in short breaths, concentrated on taking them in, and Tough watched his toiling profile with something like respect, finally. Ashen and maimed he might have been, but at that moment he knew with absolute clarity what he wanted. Tough could only imagine what that felt like.

CAMPING

The river in flood is close-up, bright brown, and in an exhilarating hurry. Nathan and I join the townspeople lining the bridge. We point at cows stranded on grassy islands. We track the progress of tree trunks being rolled. It's a competition which is the biggest, all the way to the churn at the river mouth. A line of four-wheel drives crawl the breakwater. Nathan asks a man with his daughter in his arms, when was the last time it was this bad, and where did they cop it? Not for years, he says. The Mokihinui, out country, that flooded, too. They copped it up at Seddonville – big mess up there.

We go that way anyway because we're booked in for a night. The roads are so empty we could be survivors of a sci-fi disaster. For the first stretch, the coast is hidden off to the left on the other side of the farmland. On our right, inexplicable roads break off into the hills. We drive back and forth over level crossings. I rifle through the contents of the glove box and eat a service station muffin, half listening to the news. We're not alone, apparently. The newsreader says holidaymakers in Nelson and on the Queen Charlotte Track are copping it too. The same rain is to blame. We're passing the band rotunda at Granity when the news gives way to a couple of decades-old tunes. 'Let's kill the radio,' Nathan says. I peel my feet off the dashboard and plug in my iPod. I actually don't mind old pop, listening to it is like visiting my thirteen-year-old self, but I'm not sure that Nathan does nostalgia. He configured my iTunes from his when he gave me the iPod and I've only recently started loading my own music. My old CDs, including the wistful pop, will be staying in their cases, in their boxes, in my mother's spare room.

'This is the one I told you about,' I tell him. 'The *Jump* soundtrack.'

'The annoying synth.'

'That's the one.' I press play.

After Ngakawau the coast pulls up beside us and sticks around. The beaches are stonier up here and Nikau palms stand up in front of the water. We turn inland before the Mokihinui River, into a sunny nowhere of paddocks, where beards of grass hang off the fence wire and a bone-grey silt coats the bush up to where the water reached. Seddonville looks like a garage sale cooperative: ranch sliders, front doors, garage doors are open; beanbags slouch on driveways, cardboard boxes are lined up on trampolines. I watch it all through the car window. 'Don't stare,' Nathan says. 'It's not a zoo.' A trailer-load of wet books rattles past. A few bundles of pages fall off and stay behind. We drive past a poster wrapped around a power pole, *Don't Dam the Mokihinui!* As we cross the pub car park I pick up a gritty children's reader, sixties vintage, *The Starship*. It isn't as though anyone has died. The pub's Christmas tree is laid sideways on a stack of tables and chairs. An occasional table, complete with doily and information brochures, is pushed into the gravel at the bottom of the steps.

The publican appears from a door behind the bar like the resident ghost who doesn't know he's dead. Blu-Tacked to a shelf at his shoulder is a card with a scrolled border; YOUR DUTY MANAGER in printed font, and under that, in marker pen, 'Carol'. One of the figurines on the shelf is a moneybox: a boy bent over with his pants pulled down and a slot between his butt cheeks. Nathan says something sympathetic about the damage. 'Yep, water got into our units. I phoned them at the camping ground. Be getting bloody full down there, but they said they'd take you. Have you got a tent?'

I wander over to the wall, the carpet oozing under my feet, while Nathan listens to directions. In a row of black-and-white photos, groups of olden-day men in hats pose in front of a tent, in front of a railway carriage, in front of a complicated wooden contraption. 'What's the poster about?' I hear Nathan ask. 'Don't dam the Mokihinui.'

'Greenies,' the guy says. 'Hydro scheme planned for up the river here.'

The relationships I imagined having when I was thirteen had a certain something my real relationships have lacked, several certain somethings: pregnant eye contact, extravagant surprises, rolling over each other in slow-motion. Real life provided the set-up. Was

90

there an obstacle to overcome? Was he a pen pal living in New Caledonia? Did he live only a few kilometres away but think of me as a friend? It didn't matter. I could superimpose his face onto a towel-clad American celebrity. I could survive on a dream for a week. He had neglected me out of selfless dedication to his sick sister. He attended to important male social obligations I didn't understand. The ending? Usually we'd be thrown together alone and in a heightened emotional state, probably a civil defence emergency. The kissing and rolling would follow, eventually dissolving into the blank of my inexperience. And that was it – *The End*. Screw the happily ever after. If the people who wrote the stories found it too boring to expand on, I wasn't interested either.

Two girls – denim short-shorts and tank tops and tans – join us in the barbecue area at the camping ground. They'd planned to go white-water rafting today, they tell us, but the river was still too high. The one who does most of the talking has an English accent and the other is possibly Israeli. Some variety of Middle Eastern, minus the headscarf. Bush, sea, and sky sprawl out around us. The sun is still insisting on being hot. 'I've done that rafting trip,' Nathan says. 'The one on the Lyell, right?'

'Yeah, what's it like?'

'It's good.' He pushes our crackers and pesto towards them. 'You can jump out and ride one of the small rapids in your lifejacket, if you're up for it.'

The English girl reaches forward. 'I'd be up for it.'

I hold a red onion still with one hand and chop with the other. 'Did you hear they're going to dam the Mokihinui?'

I say. 'For hydroelectric power. A whole valley will be submerged.'

'I can't believe they'd want to fuck with this environment,' the English girl says.

'It would stop the flooding, though.' Nathan is opening the valve on the barbecue's gas tank. 'Like they had at Seddonville. They could control the flow.'

'Did you see Seddonville?' she says. 'It's no great loss.' The other girl worries at the cuticles on one hand.

I expect Nathan to defend Seddonville, but he only twists a knob and presses the ignition button. 'Do you think our beers will be cold?'

'I'll check, shall I?' I lift my legs one by one over the seat of the picnic table. It isn't until I put my arm down that I realise how long I've been holding it up against the sun. It's aching.

'Are you students, or – what will you do when you get home?' I hear Nathan ask. 'Military service,' the Israeli girl says.

We had our first proper argument over a DVD. It started in the rental store. We went off in different directions and caught up to each other in the passageway with the infinity mirror and the Hollywood lights. I still didn't have anything. He held up a revenge thriller, *Unlawful Methods*. 'What?' he said.

'Nothing,' I said.

'Come on, there's something.'

'It just looks shit.'

'Can you try to explain what's putting you off?'

'I feel like watching something less intense.' We split off

and came together at least two more times before we hired a comedy about a roadie who has to pose as the lead singer of a band. When I read the back cover for the second time in the car, the premise bothered me more than it had in the store. I didn't say anything. I put the case down at my feet.

'What?' Nathan said. He drove around the block, stopped in front of the store again, and switched off the engine. When I came back out with a political satire the car was gone.

Nathan turned out to be a runner-off, a door-slammer. I pick fights to get out of things. I lit a cigarette in the car en route to his parents' silver wedding anniversary when he was three days into giving up. Spectacular gestures during fights: a friend of mine took all of her boyfriend's records out of their sleeves and baked them at 200 degrees Celsius for thirty minutes. In the end I waited outside the DVD store for fifteen minutes. We didn't speak in the car. When we got back to his flat he slapped the DVD down on the coffee table like a piece of evidence. He told me I pretended to be worldly when I had never travelled anywhere further than Sydney. He told me it embarrassed him when I was snobbish in front of his parents, who had been dealt bad luck in their lives and done well with what they had. Did I ever listen to any music I hadn't appropriated off someone else? And why was I so passive? When was the last time I'd tried something new? All in all, I didn't think he was being fair. How could I have known which parts of myself to hide until I knew which parts he'd disapprove of? I don't know what he saw in my face, but he said, 'I don't want to break up with you.'

I said, 'I don't want to break up with you either.'

'I love you,' he said.

'I love you too.' Since then I've made more of an effort to address my shortcomings. For my something new I suggested a road trip.

I'm hearing voices filtered through nylon and tent zips being drawn. I can smell trapped breath and crushed grass. When someone shines a torch outside I see it as a dipping, swinging moon. I knead my pillow and turn over. I notice that my wrist is cocked, so I straighten it. I think to relax my jaw. I tunnel a hand into my sleeping bag and scratch my lower back. I think of a lymphatic disease I've read about that's supposed to cause itchiness. I shrug my arms out and reach back to bring Nathan's hand over and clasp it with mine on my chest, but his fingers buzz around my nipples like flies, even when he's asleep, so I pick his wrist up and move it away again. A showreel of recently stored images, like looking out the car window – stony beaches and waves (I can hear them), dumps of flood debris beside the road. Whether I'm conscious or not, my brain will keep playing them, freestyle but with the same force, endlessly all night and forever, for years. The thought exhausts me, but I still don't sleep.

I borrowed a book once that claimed to show you step-by-step how to train your cat to walk on a lead. On my way home from the library, bouncing my palm off fence palings, plucking leaves off shrubs, clicking my tongue, I was already planning where I might take my cat, what we would do as a pair. Step 1 instructed me to fit a collar with a lead adjustment. Step 2: 'Attach a lead to the collar and leave the cat to trail it around.' The final step was disappointing. 'Pick up the end of the lead, slowly. Your cat shouldn't feel restricted. If she objects, drop the lead immediately.' Essentially, I was being told to *follow* my cat as she went about her business. At Step 2, Moneypenny attacked the lead and climbed the woodpile onto the garage roof. In her own sweet time she crouched and leapt towards the ground again, snagging the lead on the trellis so we had to rescue her from breaking her neck.

I delay going to the toilet. It's worth the health risks associated with bladder retention not to have to sit up, wriggle to the end of the airbed, find my hoodie and the torch, lift my hips to get out of the sleeping bag, and work my feet into cold jandals. I haven't heard any tent zips for a while, just the occasional night bird and the waves. I feel as though part of me is still back at Seddonville. One of the roads leading off nowhere from the main stretch was called Halcyon Street. When I finally drag myself into full consciousness and sit up, Nathan reaches forward and grabs one of my hands. I tell him I have to pee and he lies down again. In the tents nearby anyone who's still awake hears our tent zip go up and down, and I straighten into the outside world.

From the toilet block I can see down to the river mouth in a low contrast, soft-focus version of black-and-white. The water is still high, but there are sandbanks exposed now and massive snarls of driftwood. My watch light tells me it's two a.m., but a fire glows up from the beach and I can see people down there. I think I recognise two sets of bare legs reflecting the flames. They'll remember this and take it back around the world with them. One might mention it over a pub table and the other in the cab of an army truck: 'We lit this beach fire on the South Island one night,' they'll say. They might or might not remember the walls of wood where the river came out, or the flood that formed them. They might or might not wonder if the dam was ever built, the valley inundated, and Seddonville saved from further disasters.

I might or might not end up with Nathan. I don't think I will, but I couldn't say why exactly. What is 'ending up with' someone, anyway? Is it like an adaptation of musical chairs? Whoever you're sitting next to when the music stops?

A STRANGE STORY

I conducted my first interview with Constance Hector at the Nelson Gaol on 17th October, 1866, after the jury had retired. My position then was Editor of the *Rutherford Times*. As one would expect, I found Mrs Hector in no small degree of distress. We were seated in her primitive cell, she on the cot with her belongings in a holdall beside her and I on a stool opposite. Her attire was then and had been for the duration of the trial in a less than auspicious state. The local tendency towards practical dress notwithstanding, there were signs of disrepair about her garments, though they seemed to have been well made originally. Mrs Hector gazed at her surroundings, the bare boards and the grille – the carpentry was more rudimentary than even we are accustomed to in our hastily assembled township.

Her first words to me were, 'I studied the rooms of fashionable people, their furnishings and ornaments and so on, when I was a child. My mother brought back illustrated papers from the house where she was employed, and I pored over them for hours.' There was a helplessness to her demeanour such as a domestic animal might display in a rushing stream. One's impulse must be to reach out and pull the poor creature from the water. It was for this reason that I offered Mrs Hector some modest remuneration in return for writing this account, a proposal she agreed to. The story of her journey began on a platform at Clapham Junction, where she read a poster calling for settlers to the South Pacific colony of New Zealand. She couldn't have known the philosophical distances she would travel.

• • •

A Journey

My husband Reuben departed two months earlier than I, to establish himself and secure our accommodation. Nothing could have prepared me for the strangeness of making the sea journey without him. We single women were shut below deck by a constable and mothered by a Mistress of the Mess, while the men were free to hold concerts or wash at the pumps on deck. The single women went to some lengths to gain occasional glimpses of the young men; many of whom, it was true, seemed very fast. Whether it was the bruises we suffered by being thrown against tables and door handles, the clatter of tin crockery at night, or the stink of bilge water, there was no escaping our situation. As for the stalwarts of nautical authority, the doctor was usually drunk and the captain thought nothing of altering our schedule at a whim. I witnessed a pot of scalding coffee thrown across a new infant's head and face. The doctor provoked fresh screams when he poured cold water over the baby to effect a remedy. A clutch of girls made as if to faint at the sight of it, and he threatened to drench them also. I began to wonder if he didn't treat every complaint using this method.

What a relief to be reunited with Reuben at Hokitika, but what startling light and noise. We followed the coast, our progress dictated by the tides and, at river mouths, by the availability of punts. From Westport we kept on north to the new diggings, where I first encountered stands selling spirits or spades or Hunter's Tonic while floorboards were being nailed down behind them. This combination of otherworldly scenery and a kind of stage-prop architecture was especially disorientating. We stopped outside a makeshift inn on one such stretch where travelling diggers were spread out, resting, some of them in their cups. Foam flew up from the beach. Drunkenness was a good sign, Reuben told me – good for business. He sold five pairs of boots off the back of the coach. Afterwards, encouraged, we crossed the reeds towards the sand.

I saw the Scot for the first time propped against a length of driftwood. I wondered that his heart pumped blood all the way around his body, he was so tall, and his hair was standing up in shapes, matted with salt air and dirt. He shaded his eyes to look up at us – a pale and freckled hand with long fingers. Reuben crouched opposite him. Ten yards or so beyond, a dog waded into the foam, sniffed some into its nostrils, and snapped its jaws. 'This is far from horrible, as a place to stop,' Reuben said. There was no reply, so Reuben turned to watch the dog for a moment. 'Come from Otago, have you?'

'Didnae . . . Chasin' colour.' The man was obviously drunk. He spoke with the false starts and diversions of an insect picking its way out of a wet basin. The dog approached with a beard of dirty white and shook itself. Reuben leaned away and I took a step backwards, but the digger didn't see it happen, only investigated the foam on his shirt a few seconds later.

'You must have difficulty finding boots in your size,' Reuben said.

The man winced. His boots were scuffed and weathered, but looked in reasonable condition. 'I leave . . . elves.' He laughed.

'My name's written on this piece of paper. I'll be in Rutherford. That's what it says there, Rutherford.'

'I can. Dannae. Who?' There was a gap between his front teeth. A gap such as that always makes a person look young in spirit, somehow – both mischievous and harmless. How can that be? In any case, Reuben turned me away from the gaze the man was giving me.

'I can make a pair of boots for you if you come to Rutherford. Keep that paper.'

'Keep tha,' the man said.

I saw a number of diggers on Main Street carrying or dragging whatever they had been able to salvage in sodden bundles of canvas. I even saw a man with battered limbs on a stretcher of branches lashed together. Blood and mud had congealed on his mates' arms. When I got back to the cabin Reuben was preparing to leave down the gorge road to ask after a shipment of leather. The worst was over, they were saying, the road was passable. 'I'll be months waiting for insurance,' he told me, buttoning his coat. 'Better to see what I can recover.' He was concealing something, showing the outward signs of a concern he was keeping from me. I laid my hand on his shoulder.

'Will you be careful?' I said.

He lifted my hand from where it rested and pressed it between his own. His hands were warm. They were always warm. 'I'll bring something back for you,' he said.

A representative from the public works committee told me that a season of inundation had weakened the banks of the river. The accident was unavoidable, inevitable. Reuben was crossing over in that vile contraption when it happened; he and another man, a contractor at the battery. The cage would have been swaying above the river that sickening way it does. Reuben would have been focused on the task, peering up at the wire, pulling the slack back through the pulley, keeping his strokes even and trying not to dislodge his hat. The water was eddying under them, brown and thick with flotsam. Then the overhead wire loosened off. Reuben's efforts got them nowhere for a stroke. He might have said something. They might have seen the tree slump forward, lurched once, and then felt the give. I wonder if their stomachs dropped, how their nerves leapt. Were there shouts? Did urgent human voices follow him down? I don't like to think of a hope that might have surfaced for a few gasping seconds with his fractured bones and broken skin. I tell myself his head found a rock, just beneath the surface.

In the following weeks I was granted rest occasionally at night, when my mind would reach a kind of plateau, suspended between sleep and wakefulness. I had emerged from some terrible deeper darkness, I sensed, and I would return to it, but in those rare moments I enjoyed a peaceful oblivion. When I was awake, I remembered time and time again. I forgot instead the events of the days I inhabited. I would cut a slice of bread, make a pot of tea, then thread a needle and begin mending a torn sleeve while the bread lay uneaten and the tea went cold.

There are particular aspects of the funeral I recall. My stomach smarting and turning in on itself while we followed the coffin up the side of the gully. The way the damp earth under our feet seemed to breathe, to exhale warm air. The pallbearers sweating at the temples, straining when they had to tip the box to mount the steps to the terrace. The moment, on the hour, when they lowered him into the ground, and the battery stopped crushing. A bellbird sang into that silence. I remember seeing Abe there, at the edge of the mourners in the murk under a black beech.

The hatter Abe had come to Reuben for new boots in the few weeks before the accident. He was smoking beside the workshop while Reuben cut the leather and saw me struggling with a chicken at the back of the cabin. He put his pipe down at his feet, walked over, whistling, took the chicken from me, pulled the head down, and twisted it. The bird didn't squawk at all, only flapped about when its neck was broken. When it was still, Abe moved a few paces away from the house, laid the chicken on the ground, pulled the knife from his belt, and drew it swiftly across the neck to let the blood. He wiped the knife on a damp tuft of grass while he waited for the initial flow to ebb, then stepped onto the chopping block to string the body up from one of the beams over the woodpile. 'Leave that there for a while,' he said, and went back to retrieve his pipe, while the creature bled out.

Mrs Storm, the proprietor of the Welcome Inn, didn't waste any time. She approached me after the funeral when we stepped out of the enclosure of the trees. She had forgone her usual jewellery and colours.

She asked me, I couldn't believe it, 'Did your husband leave much stock?'

I was so surprised that I answered her. He had sold his existing stock and was expecting materials, I said.

She spoke on, almost as though she had anticipated my reply. 'I need help with the linen you see.'

I wasn't familiar with the gold-town hotels, but I needed an income, and the physical labour might calm my mind, so I nodded.

She picked up my hand – 'Stop by on Thursday' – and crossed back to the beginning of Main Street.

Abe approached then and mumbled his sorries. He didn't meet my eye but pressed something towards me, a flask of liquor. He could only open his hand, clawlike, to the halfway point to release it. 'Keep it,' he said. 'You'll need it.'

It was only one of a series of unreal-seeming events, so I took it from him, stepped into the shade and drank a mouthful, then another.

A Spree

I suppose it started on the day when Mrs Storm called me into the public bar from the side entrance, asked me to sit, and offered me beer. The shopkeepers and the postmaster patronised one of the taverns on Main Street. The men playing billiards at the Inn were shift workers from the Midas Company. I watched a pair of boots cross the rug and stop. One lifted off the floor to allow its wearer a greater reach over the table. Reuben had spent weeks manufacturing their boots before the battery opened: ten eyelets tall, his stamp inside the tongue, deep-tread soles. The previous day I had received a letter from the bank that revealed the full extent of Reuben's indebtedness. I had known almost nothing of his financial affairs.

'They'll all be on their Friday spree tonight,' Mrs Storm said. Her hair was tightly wound for daytime business, which called for acquaintance not only with her own financial affairs, but those of others. 'One of my girls is ill, and I need extra help.'

Beer had dulled the pain in my arms. They hung from my shoulders as a dead weight. The warmth from the fire and the glints from the glass in her necklace had lulled me into a sense of wellbeing.

'What would you have me do?' I said. I had seen her 'girls' in the bar, grotesque in their rouge. She poured more beer into my glass.

'Your own drinks are free,' she said. 'I wouldn't have you dancing. There'd be the bar between you and them.'

'I have no –'

'I do. I'll make you fancy,' she said.

I suffered Mrs Storm's appraisal. It transpired that Mistress of the Wardrobe was another of her roles. 'That overskirt is good with our bodice,' she said. My costume consisted of a crinoline from her, my own petticoats, a satin underskirt she had given me 'for display', and my own skirt as the outermost layer. She couldn't afford the fabric to put her girls into the new bustles, she told me, but she hooked up and fixed my overskirt to show the satin underneath. I was wearing a bodice that she had matched for colour as best she could. My skirt was a duller navy against her peacock blue. 'Anyone could see you've had that corset fitted,' she said. 'There's not many around here make a line like that.'

A column of sunlight reached through the leaf cover and in the window, revealing everything in too much detail: Mrs Storm, who looked as though she had been stuffed and sewn into her clothes; my own bare arms at five in the afternoon. I hadn't worn a crinoline for months. I had tried to push through the doorway before remembering to tilt. There was comfort in its shape, though – something of the feeling of the city. There was solace, too, in the powder and paint. When Mrs Storm handed me a looking glass, I saw in it a slightly different person than myself, someone gaudy and joyless, but with fewer concerns. This new face dealt only with what was immediately in front of it.

'It's my belief the flames won't lick around your ankles if you have a moment or two of fun,' Mrs Storm said.

The hatter Abe had a regular place at the bar. There was always a wash of noise, a backdrop of voices, and somewhere amongst it a piano being played. The smell was a blend of spilled spirits, wood and tobacco smoke. I would forget about the world outside the tavern, until each new arrival pulled the door open. The black hills would lurch towards us: they made me think of fairy tale forests, but not the fairy tales I knew. If I were alone in those dark hills, I could call until I lost my voice and the only response would be a foreign language of clicks and trills. I would die there. Birds I didn't know the names of would plant their strange feet on my bones. When the door shut again I had only to cope with the men in front of me, but that was enough.

The sun and moon chased each other through the sky. I saw more and more of the night-time and its inhabitants and less and less of the days. When two of the general stores called in debts, I began to avoid Main Street and walk past the saddlers instead to meet up with the gully track. I developed a habit of keeping my head bowed when I had to pass through town, so I never saw any reactions or knew what anyone thought of me.

Earlier that night, the night it happened, a clean-shaven man in a white collar walked into the Inn and crossed himself. 'Peace be to all here,' he said. The Irish sank to their knees. He removed a piece of folded meat-wrap from around his neck. 'Swallow your glasses, ye sorry bunch of micks.' He put the paper on the bar.

Mrs Storm nodded at it. 'You've a bloodstain on your collar, Father.'

I helped myself to a drink. A punt operator told me he'd seen two corpses in the water that morning with the eyes pecked out. I saw Reuben, eyeless, floating on the current.

Long after most of the drinkers had settled in, another pair of boots crossed the platform, another hand pulled the door open and the night poured in again – the mist the world came out of. This new arrival had to bend to clear the doorframe. I had seen the man before. It was the Scot Reuben had spoken to on the beach those months earlier. Abe also turned to watch.

'Do you know him?' I asked.

'I've seen him a couple of times,' Abe said. 'He's difficult not to see.' Most of the men in the tavern would be confronted with his chin first, a few with his neck.

The man arrived beside Abe without offering his hand. 'I know you?' he asked me.

'My husband was a bootmaker,' I said. 'He gave his card to you near Westport.' I had been sipping since the early evening and my voice was louder than I'd intended.

'It was your husband in the cage that fell?'

'Yes it was.'

'Shame.' He looked down. 'These boots are worn through.' He asked Abe, 'Who makes your boots?'

'Can't remember,' Abe said. He pushed off the bar and into the thicket of tables to one of the Irish parties. When he pulled his chair in, one or two of the men looked back.

The Scot remained in the same position, staring. 'Martell's please, and one for yourself.'

His eyes were pale. His hair, not so matted now, was a dark auburn. He looked to have quite the wrong complexion for gold-seeking. He had been a cabinetmaker in Edinburgh, he told me, but I don't remember that he talked a great deal. It had been a long time since I had indulged my interest, so I spoke at length about the styles of furnishings I admired. His way of staring seemed to disregard whatever I said, but something in my manner seemed to amuse him.

By the time Mrs Storm leaned in close and told me to take myself off, the fire was dying and she was preparing to empty the tavern of its dregs. Most of the remaining men were overnight guests, and had only the staircase to negotiate. The table where Abe had been sitting with the Irish party was empty. I hadn't noticed him leave. He usually walked home with me. 'They're probably upstairs playing cards,' she said. She nodded towards the Scot. 'No one much is going to bother him. Why don't you let him walk you?'

The Scot tapped his empty glass down on the bar. 'Will you sell me a bottle of that?'

When I woke the next morning, I couldn't remember going to bed. I waited for the memories to catch up to me, dressing myself in stages, resting on the bed in between times, clammy, moving my head around to avoid the ache.

I made my way carefully into the other room and saw someone there, leaning over a pot. I reached for a chair and sank into it. I smelled boiling meat and noticed with my usual embarrassment that the hem on the curtains had come unstitched, and that the table was scratched and sticky.

I remembered then that we had paused on the post office porch and the Scot had shown me the constellations thick in the southern sky, but they had swooped and dived when I tried to focus. I had put a capful on the dog's tongue and the dog had shaken its head.

The door was shut and the steam was dense, but I could see by his stature and the shape of his beard that it was Abe beside the stove. He tried a few cupboards for a cup, found one, and put it on the table, poured from a bottle of whisky. 'A cure. You'll need it.' I heard a dog whining outside. I'll confess now that it wasn't the first occasion I had woken up with Abe there in the cabin, but I could sense that this time was different, that I would be best to stand up, turn around, and go back to bed rather than remember, because once I had remembered, I would remember again and again. 'That dog's hungry,' Abe said.

On the back step of the cabin, I had shaken my head no, he couldn't come in. My earrings had swung back and forth, brushing my cheeks. The stars had veered past my eyes. Drunkenness was a good sign, Reuben had said that day on the beach. The Scot gripped my wrist and jerked me away from the door. He kept hold of me, though I fell.

• • •

According to Mrs Hector's nearest neighbour, there was little discernible activity in or around the cabin in the days following the killing. He only knew by seeing lamplight and chimney smoke that the cabin was inhabited at all. His horses took to shying away near the place where the Scot's body was eventually discovered, but two weeks passed before the stench prompted further investigation.

The reading public will know by now that Mr Abel Newsome, who wrote letters to Mrs Hector during the trial that indicated a strong infatuation, was found guilty of manslaughter. Constance Hector, who was charged with being an accessory after the fact, was found innocent. Those present at the trial, however, heard the judge advise her to reflect upon the unfortunate relaxation of her moral standards. I strongly believe it has been Mrs Hector's goal to avoid reflection in general for these months passed. Her account suggests a descent caused by grief, the same way a theft might be caused by poverty. I am a newspaper man, not a judge. But if I hold, due to my professional standing, any influence over public opinion, I urge tolerance of this woman. She is, after all, only one amongst the fallen.

HOME GROWN

Melissa was taken prisoner while she was walking home from the dairy. Sunshine was bouncing off the side mirrors of cars and throwing heat up from the footpath. Rex Love stepped up onto the brick wall that bordered his family's front lawn as they walked past. 'What have you got?' He was a freckled eclipse. Melissa could just feel the weight of two coins in the pocket of her shorts. He lunged and she started running. They ran over a water toby, past the neighbours' fence, and past the rise where a tree pushed up through broken edges of concrete. He caught up to her at the honeysuckle on the corner, pulled her arms behind her back, and held them there while they both caught their breath. She didn't have the will to escape. The touch of his hands on her wrists was interesting. He smelled of something he must have been playing with in the garage, something out of a tin he'd had to pry open. 'You're a prisoner,' he said, and steered her back past the tree and through the shadows of the fence towards the sprinkler that was flicking over a bleached patch of their front lawn. Someone in the next section was revving a chainsaw. Then Melissa saw it – the dyed mist, like the air-brushed technicolour in toy catalogues. 'Hey, rainbow!' she shouted. Rex loosened his grip. And Melissa's sister grabbed him from behind.

Almost thirty years later, Rex sent Melissa a friend request on Facebook. They sent a few messages back and forth, swapped a few memories. The sprinkler rainbow was one. He owned a bach he rented out, he told her. The location was to-die-for – surrounded by bush, a private river beach across the road. He uploaded photos of a lagoon-like setting and a window-seat. He suggested that Melissa might like to take some time off and get away from it all. In her messages, she'd gone into detail about a few of the things and people she'd like to get away from. She began to get excited. She wanted to get back to the holiday feeling from all those years ago, when peace had been boring and she'd dreamed of being struck by tragedy and inheriting a Californian mega-mansion. She pictured herself relaxing in the window-seat with a jigsaw puzzle. Her sister agreed with the idea of a holiday, in principle.

After the last pit-stop town on the eastern side of the Alps, her progress took on a drifting quality. Hills pushed up under the car, outcrops of limestone loomed over the road, then the vista opened out to riverbeds, broad terraces and shingle fans – fence wire and flowering gorse. An approaching ute flashed its lights in the sun. Melissa didn't understand why. She climbed higher, past the Engineer's

Camp to the top of the pass, up among the peaks. Her stomach clenched at the sheer drop beside the road. As she steered her way through beech forest down into the West Coast, the winter leaves scattered over the road like bronze confetti.

It was early evening when she frisked the back of the shed for the key. She found a Stinking Iris growing along the path and snapped some of the pods off. Looking at photos of the place online, she'd easily been able to imagine people just out of shot or in different rooms. She'd at least sensed somebody behind the lens. But now she nosed from vacant living room into vacant kitchen, bathroom and bedrooms. It had been an abrupt switch – the state highway dipping and rising under the car, the bush blurring on either side, and then the bumping over potholes in the unsealed road, being able to hear the crunch of aggregate under the wheels, to pick out individual branches and leaves. The place was so complete in itself and so unfamiliar – the nautical fabric on the padded bench seat in the window, the bathmat with the suction cups – that she didn't know where to settle. Instead of a puzzle on the table she found a note. 'Hot water switched on. Come for a meal tomorrow night. Rex.' When he was a kid, Rex's lips had always been too wet. His uncle had featured in a Reader's Digest real-life survival story after his parachute didn't open. Melissa spent the night with the TV on for company, splitting Stinking Iris pods open with her thumbnail and pushing out the orange seeds, while the bars of the radiant heater burned off dust.

Rex's was the last in a row of cribs at the river mouth. He was standing at his ranch slider when she pulled up. She wouldn't have recognised him if she'd glanced at him on the street. He was gaunt and long-jawed. His lips had dried out. Behind him, the porch was cluttered with plywood, rolls of plastic sheeting, and a torn sofa. 'You made it,' he said. 'Drive okay?'

'No problem.' A poodle cross with a cloud of grey fur drifted out to the porch, tottering on its back legs. When it butted into Rex, he picked it up and half threw it past Melissa out the door. She bent down and held her hand out. The dog sniffed in her direction but then seemed to lose its train of thought.

'Blind. He had a stroke a few years ago,' Rex said. He held a rice paper open and pinched for tobacco in his pouch.

• • •

Rex snapped a handful of dried spaghetti in half and dropped it into the pot. He picked up a pre-rolled joint from the table and lit it. 'Go on, then, Satan. Why don't you piss on the floor.' That's what the dog was doing. He was pissing on the lino. Rex got up and rummaged under the sink for a rag, dropped it onto the puddle, and pushed it around with his foot. He kicked it in the direction of the washing machine then came back and poured two glasses of wine. Melissa checked her phone for coverage – definite bars. She was breathing in a thick aroma of garlicky tomatoes blended with weed. Satan nosed at his food bowl then wandered over and got tangled in the legs of her chair.

She rested her fingers on the base of her wine glass and a rectangle of crimson light spilled from her hand onto the tablecloth.

They were a few mouthfuls in when he started. 'So look, I'm going to tell you something,' he said. 'It might blow your mind. It blew my mind.' He put down his fork and picked up his rice papers. 'I've been reading these books. The author's done shitloads of research. Academic credentials for Africa.' His teeth were beginning to stain from the wine. 'There was a certain point, see. A certain point in ancient history when everything changed.' Melissa was half listening and half staring at the Dali print behind him on the wall. She'd never seen the elephant on giant stilt legs in the background before. 'The way this guy sees it,' Rex was saying, 'Homo sapiens had help evolving. It's all marked down on these tablets. They created us to work for them.' She felt the same way about her wine as she did about her meal – concerned that it had been contaminated by dog piss somehow.

'They wanted to get at the earth's resources. Who, is the question. Who are *they*? It's too complicated to explain all at once.'

When he got up to take their plates to the bench she keyed in a text to her sister. Rex didn't notice what she was doing, even when she had to find the exclamation mark. 'Look into this stuff though, seriously: the Sumerians used this word *Annunaki*: "those who from heaven to earth came".'

'Yeah I will,' she said, and sent the message. 'Hey, what's your uncle been up to? The one who had the accident.'

Rex opened the fridge and took out a Sara Lee box. 'He

had a bodybuilding gym in Chiang Mai. Fucked his body up with steroids. Hey, can you keep a secret?'

Melissa didn't want to keep any of Rex's secrets, and her sister was always telling her she didn't establish clear enough boundaries, but she didn't actively object.

'Before we have dessert, do you want to see my growing room? Hydroponic.' He opened a slatted door and pulled a cord. A fluoro strip light lit up the first few treads of a set of stairs leading underground. 'I have a lot of those,' he said, pointing to the strip, 'but bigger, with four tubes on each unit. For the extra lumins.' Apparently she'd missed her opportunity, boundary-wise. When had that been?

'I feel like Alice.' She was holding on to the rail at the top of the steps. Rex was behind her. 'Careful,' he said. After taking a few steps, she was looking down on rows of reflector hoods. This was no one-man kitchen garden. There were easily fifty plants. The lights were buzzing.

'Who dug this out?' she asked.

'It was here when I bought the place. With only a ladder though. I had to put the stairs in.'

'Actually, I'd better – I'm expecting a call.'

'Who from?' he said. He even lifted his arms away from his sides to block her way.

'Why?'

'I just wanted to show you,' he said. 'It took ages to set up.' He licked his lips, but it didn't make any difference. 'All right, we don't have to.'

Later, when Satan had fallen asleep in his basket, Melissa said, 'Do you think you know who you really are, Rex?'

'We can't look at ourselves directly. We're like suns, too bright.'

'You spend a lot of time on the internet, don't you?'

'Everything I need is on there.'

'*He* never looked at me directly, that's for sure.'

'It is good to talk to someone, though.'

'Like a moon. No light of his own, he just reflects other people's.' She sent another text to her sister. It said, Thank you for shining.

'The thing is, these days I have this – it's like a cloud over my soul.'

A lion's roar. Her sister had texted back, What? RU OK? Melissa looked into Rex's eyes and yes, she could see the shadow there. He had more to say. She could see it coming, as though he was going to be sick. Whatever she had been expecting, this was very far from it. 'I'm sorry, I have to go. My sister's been trying to reach me.'

This time he didn't protest. He just walked over and opened the door. She was free to go.

'It's not just your cloud, Rex,' she said, getting up from her seat. 'Not just your soul.'

MAGGIE QUINN

Mrs Quinn was Margaret Quinn but would always be known as Maggie. I sometimes overheard my parents when they thought they were speaking in private. They usually put a 'poor' in front of her name. Poor Maggie Quinn. Poor Mrs Quinn had no family of her own, only a dead husband and the care of the Beaches' children from 8.30 until dinner time. I was her assistant. Each day before the sun climbed out from behind the rocky shelves of the Alps, I'd cross next door in the boom of the waves to the schoolhouse. I'd turn my head away if the wind was throwing drizzle across my face, as it often was. I'd light the stove and linger there in the stuttering glow, between two rows of curtainless windows. When I crossed back the sky would already be growing lighter. Day would emerge from night as though from deep water.

The day the rocks arrived for the grotto was also Sarah Dingle's birthday. She arrived at school late, wheezy and cake-laden, and explained in a puffing stage-whisper that her, mother had to calm, Gretel before she would give them, any milk and, we have milk not water on our birthdays, Ma says. Mrs Quinn held my gaze for a moment. The cake might have mended any offence, but Sarah kept on: 'Milk and jam on our birthdays and, cake to take.'

Mrs Quinn held her hands out for the cake and remained silent while Sarah sat down. 'I was talking about animals and their young,' she finally said. 'Of course, the period of infant dependence for humans as well as cows can be cut short for a number of reasons. During the Hunger my own mother, for example, birthdays or not, fed her own servings to us until she fell ill, rest her soul.' She crossed herself. Out of Hell and Home, most of us would rather go to Hell. Home was more terrifying because Mrs Quinn had survived to describe the details.

Later the same day, she took a lesson on the oceans. 'The sea is the water that covers much of the Earth, portions of which are named as individual oceans.' The facts she gave us never fitted together easily. 'Within the oceans are smaller seas, such as the Dead Sea.' Her voice, which had been ranging across the tables and into the high corners of the room, stopped to direct itself at one subject. 'No doubt George Healey is contemplating the sea out the window at this very moment and considering whether it's an ocean. His vast sense of wonder might cause his mouth to gape open in that gormless way.' Sarah Dingle slapped George on the back of the head. 'You!' George turned back to Mrs Quinn, expecting another onslaught from the front, but she was pointing at Sarah. That was how she was. You could be collared for taking it upon yourself as well as for opting out.

Mrs Quinn took the nursery blanket down from its hook in the corner. She sat in her chair and spread the mint-green crochet over her lap while Sarah drifted to the front of the room. Sarah knew the routine from watching other students, but when it came to her turn, she seemed newly uncertain. Mrs Quinn had to point before she sat and reclined in her place. 'The older children, please list the names of as many oceans and seas as you can. You young ones, the words "ocean" and "sea" are written on each of your slates. You're to copy them while I comfort this baby, who doesn't know how to control herself.' She had forgotten, or didn't care, that the world's major bodies of water were labelled on a world map that was hung at the front of the classroom, legible to young eyes.

Her focus instead was on the blanket, tucking it in and wrapping it around Sarah's head so only her face was visible. Her shins and feet poked out of the end and hung in midair. 'There, there, little baby.' Sarah's expression was unreadable in profile. An elbow here and a snigger there were expected of us, encouraged even, but didn't seem to disrupt Mrs Quinn's concentration. In the last few moments before she tipped Sarah from her lap and stood up to check our work, her perfunctory rocking back and forth had relaxed into a soothing rhythm. By that time I had written the names of the Atlantic, Indian, and Pacific oceans from memory, and copied down the Arctic and Antarctic, and the China and Tasman Seas.

The road, which turned in off the beach a few hundred yards north of the school, could be seen from only one seat in the back corner. Mrs Quinn preferred me to sit in this position to prevent one of the younger or worse-behaved children being distracted, and so that I could inform her about any arrivals. The other children were expected to feign indifference while, often against a backdrop of rattling wheels and shouted greetings, I rose and made my way up the front to bend over and mumble that a stranger was driving a cart of pit sawn timber, that the Superintendent's entourage was riding in, or, as I did on that day, that the load of granite had arrived for the building of the grotto.

I had stopped on the stump at the back door of the cottage that morning, my boots slanting on the rings of grain, the day surfacing in the sky. My father, I knew, would be tipping water from the firepot into a basin, submerging a cloth, burying his face in it and rubbing the back of his neck. My mother would spoon tea into the pot afterwards and lift the lid off the bread crock. 'Maggie will have somewhere for her bonnets and booties.' Her voice escaped around the edges of the door. 'Sure she didn't see fit to pass them on to someone who could use them.' Mrs Quinn had been expecting a child, had been large in the stomach when I started school, but the baby had died being born and caused her damage. The grotto was going to be set back into the bush behind the old campsite. The local priest would bless the place on one of his fortnightly Sundays and there'd be somewhere to remember the lost, especially those whose headstones had been planted back over the Pacific, Indian, and Atlantic. The first arrivals had been hoarding keepsakes from Home, combs and caps and pillboxes.

Perhaps it was no wonder then that a person could be tipping cowpats off the blade of her shovel onto the vegetable garden and chopping them apart to release the cattle stink, hearing the whoomph and crackle of a tree being felled in the bush which stretched back across plains, jumped rivers, choked gullies, smothered mountain slopes, and continued on – when a figure dressed for errands in Ennis or wearing his wedding suit would appear from behind the outhouse and glance over, proud and disorientated, before continuing out of sight around the far corner of the cottage. No wonder that when this person dropped the handle of her spade and walk-ran along the near side of the cottage, breathing burn-off now instead of dung, slowed by her skirts pushing through the thick tufts of grass, feet landing blindly on the uneven ground, there was nothing to see from the front of the house but the beach – a forlorn stretch of shingle punctured by pyres of driftwood and red reeds. The sky was indistinguishable from the mist. There was no horizon. The sea and sand were only gradations of the same grey, subtle shifts in texture and shade. The rolled arch of a wave sucked in was tone and energy, time and energy, one becoming the other.

VISITORS

Leanne got the call at dinnertime. She hustled her son into the car with the remains of his homemade burger. They were driving out in full sunshine. 'What happened?' he said. His name was Troy.

'They flew Dad to hospital in a helicopter.'

'Wicked. Would he have been able to see our house?'

'I don't know. Maybe.' One of her cousins, a paramedic, would tell her later that there had, in fact, been an amazing view of the mining operations and surrounding area from the rescue helicopter. Her husband had been unconscious and strapped to a spinal board, so he hadn't been able to enjoy it. His name was Aidan.

'Horse,' Troy said. He swallowed, in a hurry to get it out. 'Back in the paddock at the corner.'

'All right, a point for you.' She dropped Troy at Aidan's mother's and found a station playing hard rock to keep her alert for the ninety minutes to Greymouth. The volume was so high that she almost didn't hear her phone ring, this time to say that they were transferring Aidan to Christchurch.

Weekdays, Leanne had been minding two children, eighteen months and three, for a woman she'd gone to school with. The morning of the accident, the children's mother hadn't been in her usual rush when she arrived home. 'Can you stop for a cuppa?' she'd said, and pulled a quick, toothy smile. It was the same smile she'd directed at parents and teachers when they were teenagers. Leanne rested the top half of her bottom on the edge of the sofa cushion.

'I'd better not stay, Troy's with Dawn.' Dawn was Troy's grandmother.

'No worries. I should put this monkey down for a sleep anyway. I just wanted to tell you some news.'

Leanne pushed up on her hands and shifted back onto the cushion by a few inches. Standing in the woman's kitchen she would sometimes imagine that she herself drove an Audi and prepared her meals on a stainless steel worktop, the utensils hanging in a row beside the gas hob. Then she'd see Troy pulling the seatbelt in the Audi, Troy following her into the kitchen.

'We've put an offer on a house over the hill.'

'Oh wow, that's exciting.' Leanne rose and stepped forward, and they exchanged a brief hug, all arms.

'We've been thinking of doing it for a while. And now seemed like a good time, before the kids start school. We can set up a home office, run things from there.'

'Doesn't matter where you are, does it? With iPhones and –'

'It's a bit nerve-racking of course, the palaver of shifting house.'

'The kids'll be fine. They love a change of scene at that age.' She had no personal experience of moving pre-schoolers to new towns or cities.

'Are you sure I can't make you a cup of tea?'

'No, thanks, I have to keep moving.' She had, lately, gone as far as to imagine scenes between herself and the husband, owner of the Audi and the stainless steel. Occasionally the husband would drop home during the morning, to collect something or talk to a tradesman. He'd wink at her from the coat-rack when he left. Some people were winkers, she told herself. It was a kind of playfulness. Sometimes at home when Aidan was staring at the television or computer screen, Leanne would wave her hand in front of his face. 'Remember to blink,' she'd say.

After closing the car door she sat at the wheel in the driveway for a few moments. She flicked the sun visor down to look in the vanity mirror, pulled the skin of her cheeks back where it settled into creases around her mouth, then put her foot on the brake and turned the ignition, so the children's mother wouldn't see her out the window and wonder what she was still doing there.

The birthing suite in Westport had been closed during a round of funding cuts the year before Troy was born. Leanne had ridden in an ambulance to Greymouth along the Coast Road, which was one of the top ten scenic trips in the world according to a popular travel guide. In this case it was obscured from view in the back of the ambulance, but Leanne had seen it all before. Strapped in, gripping the side rails as the road wound in and out of steep-sided coves, she tried to negotiate with the student nurse, between contractions, for something stronger than the paracetamol students could administer. She felt the pain from her ribs to her knees. When Aidan and the nurse helped her through the doors at Grey Base Hospital, the receptionists were shutting down their computers. When Troy was placed pink and frowning into her arms, the obstetrician was sipping his morning coffee, smiling. Leanne reluctantly dragged her gaze away from the authority figure and down towards her son, his crop of hair still damply plastered to his head. Of all the babies she had imagined – bald, hairy, girls, boys, milk-spotted, blotchy, pink, blue – he was only this one now.

•••

When Dawn's son had the accident that paralysed him, Dawn was in the fish and chip shop. She held her mobile phone up to her ear and listened while she stared at a print-out stuck to the wall: a site safety sign hanging across the Statue of Liberty's chest that read 3 DAYS SINCE LAST MASS SHOOTING. The smell of deep fryers would always remind her.

'Knock knock,' Troy had said to her that morning.
  'Who's there?'
  'Boo.'
  'Was that supposed to be scary?'
  'No, you have to say boo who!'
  'Oh. Boo who?'

'Don't cry. It's only a joke.'

Dawn's last mouthful of toast had stuck in her throat.

'But even if it was supposed to be a fright you didn't get one.'

When she finally coughed the lump into her hand, she collected it in her handkerchief, trying not to let Troy see. Troy thought this was funny. He lost his mouthful of milk in a hiccupping spray over the rim of his plate. That was even funnier. But what really got him laughing was the plug of mucus that shot out of his right nostril. Days since last choking episode, 0.

'You know, your great granddad used to –'

He coughed wetly, swallowed. 'Cough out coal dust. I know.'

She listened to him paddle-foot across the linoleum and said to nobody, 'I'll clear this up, shall I?'

The flowers on the agapanthus along the fence exploded in clusters from their stalks. An occasional shoosh carried from State Highway 67, and next door's baby bawled minutely against whatever torture it was being subjected to – cool sheets in a darkened room, or having its fist forced into a cotton sleeve. The sun hadn't yet burned off the humidity. Troy went around lifting the mats in his obstacle course to tip off puddles, smearing the rivulets across the PVC to evaporate. He exclaimed every now and then when the surface of a mat was hotter than he'd expected. It irked Dawn how elaborate the whole thing was. Leanne had told her to think of it like one of the commando courses they did in the army. 'He's getting fit, and he's outside,' she'd said, as though she were advertising it on TV, which was appropriate because Troy's father had based it on a TV programme – the competitors took turns swinging between ropes and clinging to narrow ledges with the goal of becoming the next 'Supreme Soldier'. He didn't half carry on, Troy, reciting the competitors' names and their statistics, the costumes they wore and their signature gestures. He was obsessed with the details. Getting fit? He hardly ever actually set out around the course.

The old boy next door waved over from his tomato plants, sparrows fossicking around his kneeling bones, and Dawn nodded to him, wondering what he might have seen from his windows recently – Leanne and Aidan in sweatshirts and bare legs smoking furtive cigarettes? Drinking with friends on the patio after Troy had gone to bed? They might have tried out the course, clambered over the hurdles and dropped heavily onto the mats, lain there giggling. So what? Everyone should push the boat out once in a while. The neighbour himself had got around a bit in his day.

'In the semifinals, the fireman – he got halfway up the pole climb –' With difficulty, Troy mimed a person holding onto a pole with his legs. 'He got halfway and he went –' He pumped his fists in the air.

'Like this?' She lifted her own arms above her head, feeling the droop under her sleeves. She was missing a repeat of her favourite criminal profiler.

'Don't, Nana.'

'Shall we go visit Granddad soon?'

'Yeah okay. Just watch me go round once.'

'I'm watching.'

The tarseal glistened and steamed. Troy jerked around to look back at the Utopia Road corner. 'Weka!'

'All right, but we passed the Pollards' horse back there, when I didn't know we were playing.' One of the mining company's utes turned off ahead. The three of them had been on the visitors' tour a while back, she and Leanne and Troy – had watched the trucks beetle over the terraces like toys, out of all proportion, the coastline ribboning away a thousand feet below. Through the static and the abbreviated code, it had been difficult to decipher the messages in and out over the driver's radio, but somehow one of the men knew to give them a wave from the cab of his outsized steel body as he powered past. Aidan. Ten hours of it, seven days on. Was it any wonder they'd want to let their hair down?

In the second row from the road, at the fourth grave along, Dawn removed the week-old flowers and collected up the soggy petals that had stuck to the base. Troy crouched on the adjacent empty plot with the fresh bunch. He'd never said if it bothered him, spending all this time with his Nana: her cluelessness about his heroes, her mid-morning game shows, and the way she'd bring him here, make him poke flower stalks into a hurricane vase. She straightened and moved back off the grave, remembering how embarrassing her mother's grief had been, how the eyes would lose focus and the mouth would slacken and waver – how that had always been worse than histrionics somehow. Through a wobbling film she saw the boy's shape move towards her and felt his arms encircle her waist. She stood perfectly still, the way she might if a fantail landed on her shoulder.

• • •

Leanne drove over Arthur's. She arrived at Christchurch Public at midnight. Aidan had his own room, which worried her straight off. Even worse, it was nice. He had his own control panel, monitors and power outlets for more, around his head, which was shaved (strange, he'd been thinking of doing that anyway). At least there were none of the horror-film harnesses or halos she'd been terrified of seeing. She sat down in the chair beside the mechanised bed, meshed her hand with one of his, and rubbed the other hand along the top of her thigh, wishing she'd brought pyjamas for him. 'How's your big wheel?' she asked.

He started to smile, then didn't quite get around to it.

'What happened?'

'Fell down the stairway coming off the catwalk.' He glanced up as a nurse put a jug of water and a stack of glasses on the bedside cabinet. 'Hit the bottom step.' A cellphone rang in the corridor, scales on a piano.

'He's still mildly sedated,' the nurse said, on her way over to close the door.

The doctor was a blusher. As she started in on the explanations, scarlet blotches spread across her face. Aidan had suffered a complete spinal cord injury, she told them, causing what was likely to be permanent paraplegia. The only ongoing health problems they anticipated were secondary to lack of mobility, pressure sores for example. Paralysis was the major issue, she told them. And there was a strong likelihood of depression during the adjustment period.

This woman must have to wear sunscreen whenever she went outside, Leanne thought. She followed Aidan's gaze in the direction of a muted TV screen suspended from the ceiling on the other side of the room. It was the kind of show where the people lived their lives between a lounge and a kitchen, cracking jokes. All you could ever see when someone came to the front door was a hint of awning and unnatural light; the view through the ranch slider in the background was always obscured by a high wall or trellis, so you didn't wonder why the weather never changed.

One night Aidan had come down off the hill with two workmates, a blaster and the guy who drove the superdozer. They'd barbecued. Troy had spent most of time tracing the chevrons on the patio with the toe of his sneaker. If he'd been impressed Leanne would have known all about it later. When she'd tucked him in, he would have repeated their stories to her. He would have googled superdozers. But he hadn't done any of that. He'd asked her to move the small TV in from their room so he could watch one of his DVDs.

Once he was settled in she'd kicked back and had a few herself. Still later, Aidan had decided to go out for more bourbon. Where was he going to buy drink at one in the morning? she'd asked. She'd climbed up to sit on the bonnet of his truck and he'd given the accelerator a quick tap, just enough to send her arms flying out for purchase.

• • •

Because he failed the blood alcohol test, administered as the helicopter chopped away from the mountain, Aidan wasn't entitled to compensation for the accident. Instead, Leanne took in boarders during his rehabilitation – geologists and specialist mechanics (one who listened to machinery with a stethoscope). She displayed their photos in the hall so the guests who came after would feel more at ease, part of one big, ocean-straddling family. They spread across the wall: from Perth, from the Philippines, from Wyoming. Already unfashionable, they posed beside the giant wheels of dozers and excavators in their fluorescent vests, helmets, and safety glasses. Leanne liked the vibe they brought into the house, though: technical and scientific. Clint from Wyoming gave Troy a plumb bob, which would always show him a straight vertical line.

ACKNOWLEDGEMENTS

Thanks to Damien Wilkins and my workshop group at the International Institute of Modern Letters, Kathryn Walls, and the donor who funded my project scholarship. Thanks also to Fergus Barrowman at Victoria University Press and to Ashleigh Young.

A number of other people helped in a variety of ways, such as Rosa Koch, who spread her family history collection out on the living-room floor and sorted through it with me. I appreciate you taking the time.

Two books were especially useful: Stevan Eldred-Grigg, *Diggers, Hatters and Whores: The Story of the New Zealand Gold Rushes*, Random House New Zealand, 2008; and Philip Ross May, *The West Coast Gold Rushes*, Pegasus Press, 1962.